Alliance

Two Worlds Book #2

by Timothy L. Cerepaka

An Annulus Publishing Book

Annulus Publishing, Cherokee, Texas, 2015

Published by Annulus Publishing

Copyright © Timothy L. Cerepaka 2015. All rights reserved.

Formatting by Timothy L. Cerepaka

Contact: timothy@timothylcerepaka.com

Cover design by Elaina Lee of For the Muse Design
(http://www.forthemusedesign.com/)

ISBN-13: 978-0692524749

ISBN-10: 0692524746

Acknowledgments

I would like to thank my uncle, James Wilhite, for helping me get this manuscript into publishable shape. I'd also like to thank the rest of my family for supporting me while I wrote this novel. You guys rock.

Acknowledgements

Chapter 1

Date: Asiday, fifth day of the week, Zaxo 10th, 3050 XE, six years after the last Xeeon city election

Time: 10:00 AM XST (Xeeonite Standard Time), 10:00 PM DST (Delanian Standard Time)

Location: Ra-Dela, capital city of Se-Dela, largest and most powerful country on Dela. More specifically, in Ra-Dela's dwarfish slums, though do not have much information about this particular area, as Database records have little facts on this part of Ra-Dela, aside from noting that many violent criminals and mentally disturbed individuals of all Delanian races live here due to stigma and Se-Dela's lack of mental health resources. Best to be cautious, as records indicate that visiting Xeeonites have been known to be attacked by this slum's residents. Activating sensors to avoid being taken by surprise.

Objective: Find and apprehend wanted criminal Jornan ah Kona. She is wanted on both Dela and Xeeo for a variety of crimes. Her most recent crime is running an illegal vampire feeding ring in Xeeo, which resulted in twenty deaths total: ten humans, four elves, and six dwarves.

After completing objective, I will return to Xeeo, with Jornan in tow, where the Xeeonite High Court will judge her in accordance with the law. Doubt she will be given a light sentence, considering her long list of crimes, but it is not in my place to speculate about such matters. Only to bring to justice those who have broken the law.

I stand on top of an abandoned building in Ra-Dela's southern edge, where few people live. Sensors indicate that, through the hard wood ceiling of the warehouse, that Jornan is directly beneath my feet. Jornan is also a witch, which is how I locate her in the first place. My sensors pick up a skyras energy spike coming from this warehouse. The spike lasted thirty-six seconds, but that had proven to be more than enough time for me to confirm its source.

Daylight is low. Sun is setting in the east, making visibility difficult. Night vision senses activating, but will not receive full usage of them until the sun goes down completely. If warehouse lacks interior light, I may be able to use this earlier; if not, I will survive.

Paralysis repulser blaster—PRB for short—is at 98% power. It should have been 100%, but Portals always take a fraction of a machine's overall energy levels whenever a machine such as myself travels through them. Ninety-eight percent will work, though I must not get cocky, because Jornan is still a threat with her skyras rings, which have unknown magical properties.

Perform a quick run-down of my various programs.

Connection to Database: Lost, as the Database does not have a server in Dela. Have to rely on mobile Database, which is housed in my memory unit, though due to storage capacities is far more abridged than the full Database. Mobile Database files are 10.0.2, which means they are up to date, as 10.0.2 is the latest update for the mobile files.

Arms and legs are fully functional, though left knee squeaks slightly. Quickly fix with tiny droplets of oil from finger, but make note to bring knee to the attention of one of the certified technicians back in HQ after I return to Xeeo. My quick fix will do for now.

Optics are not obscured. Zoom in feature—which allows me to see two dwarves arguing in a building on the other side of town —works, as did zoom out feature, which returns my vision to its original size.

Alert! Audio receptors pick up sounds of feet in leather boots coming up behind me. I whirl around, aiming my PRB, only to see that it is my temporary ally in Dela, Sir Alart Garson of the Knights of Se-Dela.

Sir Alart is a tall human specimen, male, wearing typical metalligick armor that all members of the Knights wear. It covers his body from head to toe, with knobs along the shoulders, arms, and chest to allow its user to activate the skyras energy stored in it. Carries a sword by his side, a silver-white one, which I recognize as the best kind of weapon to use to kill a vampire. Quite appropriate, because records indicate that Jornan typically works with vampires and vampires cannot be killed via most normal means.

Unlike most Delanian humans, Sir Alart's left eye is mechanical, a generic type of mechanical eyeball that is popular among those who lost their eyeballs in an accident. Its pupil extends and retracts as he draws closer to me, as if he is trying find the best setting to view the situation.

"You ready for this?" Sir Alart asks. I sense tenseness in his tone.

I nod. "Of course. I have nothing to fear. I have you and the other Knights to aid me should the target prove difficult to catch."

"And you're also a robot," Sir Alart points out. "Which means you can't feel fear at all, right?"

Again, I nod. "That is correct, Sir Alart. All emotions are foreign to me, though I've found I don't need them in order to be an effective law enforcer."

Sir Alart shudders, as if I had just said something disturbing, though my reference files for human social interaction do not indicate I misspoke. "I just can't imagine it. Ruthlessly enforcing the law, without any sort of mercy or kindness behind your actions. Makes me glad we Knights are mostly organic."

Despite my lack of emotion, I begin to question just how useful an ally Sir Alart is. Most Delanians are so afraid of robots like myself that they do not talk even this much to me; even so, Sir Alart does not appear to like me that much. He seems to view our alliance the same way that the street cleaners of Xeeon view their job: an unpleasant task that needs to be completed quickly.

Were I a human, I might be offended by that; however, I am not a human. It doesn't matter to me if Alart considers me his best friend or not. What matters is that we are both law enforcers who, with luck and skill, are about to put an infamous criminal who has terrorized both of our worlds for decades behind bars.

Nonetheless, I ask, "Are the rest of the Knights in position, in accordance with the plan?"

4

"Every last one of them," Alart confirms. He gestures with his hands at the area surrounding the buildings. "They'll strike like cobras as soon as they see the signal."

"Excellent," I say. "They have the communicators I gave them?"

Alart grimaces. He pulls a tiny, handheld radio from his armor and waves it in front of me. "Yes. And they all know how to use these infernal contraptions, too, so you don't have to worry about anyone messing up."

"Good," I say, "though I notice you sound less than enthusiastic about these devices."

Alart puts his away as he says, "Because they're unnatural. The way we Knights usually remain in contact in situations like this, we either have a portal monkey to deliver handwritten notes to each other or develop a series of bird calls we can use to signal our positions to each other without giving our position away to the enemy or some other signal that only we would recognize."

"Both methods sound inefficient to me," I remark. "But it does not matter. I see that we are both armed and ready to go, so why don't we head down and find out what kind of party Jornan is throwing?"

I wait for Alart's response, but the Knight simply stares at me as if my head had popped off its sprockets and rolled at his feet.

"Was that ... a joke?" says Alart in disbelief. "From you?"

I nod and smile. "Yes. It was funny, wasn't it?"

"It was ..." Alart seems to struggle with finding the appropriate words to criticize my humor. "Why did you tell a joke? I thought bots like you didn't have a sense of humor."

"We normally don't," I explain. "But the Xeeon City

5

Government has been making a concerted effort to 'humanize' us J bots, because they are starting to think that our normal robotic selves are frightening to the citizenry."

"Uh, okay," says Alart. "But—"

"To achieve this goal, I have been downloading many electronic books on humor so I can become the funniest robot in all of the two worlds," I continue (because I feel it is important for him to understand completely what I am doing to achieve this goal). "I have downloaded books by such famous Xeeonite comedians as 'Mad-Hammer' Hagan and 'Master of Comedy' Killan. I have learned the secrets of humor from their books; in fact, Hagan's book is titled *Secrets of Humor*, appropriately enough."

Sir Alart shakes his head in exasperation. "I've never heard of either of those two comedians, but whatever. Let's just do our job. You can joke later, after we've busted Jornan and her cronies."

"An excellent suggestion, Sir Alart," I say. I tap the side of my head. "But may I suggest that you take your attitude and sell it to the Attitude Store on Sixth street? Because I hear you can make good money doing that."

Sir Alart glares at me. "What did I say about joking?"

"That joke was from Hagan's *Secrets of Humor*," I explain, because I can see that Sir Alart clearly did not 'get' the joke, as most comedians say. "Chapter three, under the section 'Jokes You Can Tell Jerks Who Can't Take a Joke.'"

"I liked you better when I thought you were just another stiff robot," said Sir Alart. He rests his sword on his shoulder, turns, and walks to the entrance leading from the roof of this building into the interior.

ALLIANCE

I follow quickly, but do not make any more jokes. This is partly because this is not the situation to be joking around in, but also because I now wonder if I 'botched' the joke, as the books say. Perhaps I need more practice, which the books say you should do if you want to become a great comedian. I have no aspirations to become a comedian—I much prefer law enforcement—but I resolve to tell better jokes nonetheless.

Sir Alart opens the door and peeks inside, even though I could just as easily have told him that there is no one in there thanks to my sensors failing to pick up any signs of life. Still, he pulls his head out and says to me, "It's safe," before disappearing within.

The door almost closes itself behind him, but I catch it with one hand and enter. We stand in a dark, narrow room, with holes in the walls, ceiling, and floor from years of neglect. My optics catch a tiny spider of undetermined species crawl into a hole on the floor, but I do not allow myself to be distracted by that, because Sir Alart and I are in the enemy territory now, which means that we have to be on high alert at all times to avoid being taken by surprise.

The ceiling is low enough that Sir Alart must crouch to avoid scraping the top of his helmet against it. I do not need to, but I do so anyway in order to avoid giving our enemies less of a visible target. Though I doubt that our enemies could harm me much; aside from Jornan, the rest of her minions do not seem to have any skyras rings of their own, which means they likely rely on old-fashioned weapons like swords and cudgels and knives, weapons that pose a tiny threat to robots like myself.

We soon emerge onto one of the two catwalks extending across the ceiling of the warehouse. We do so very slowly, because both of us are heavy, Sir Alart due to his armor, I due to being constructed entirely out of metal. We manage to make very little noise as we walk across it, but I am prepared to fight the moment someone notices u; though our keeping silent isn't entirely necessary, because below us come the loud—almost too loud—conversations of Jornan and her minions even before we see them.

Her minions are mostly dwarves, which is why my audio receptors pick up such loud and hostile tones, as my records say that dwarves generally speak in gruffer tones than most Delanian species.

"Come on, come on," says a woman's voice, which I quickly match with the audio file of Jornan's I have downloaded into my memory. It is harsh and impatient, which is a good description of the witch in general. "You dwarves are so slow. We need to get this shipment of super speed out *tonight*, and if you idiots don't get all of this packed and through the Portal soon, we'll miss our deadline and the Founder will be beyond angry."

I understand most of what she says—for example, super speed is a Delanian drug that is popular on both Xeeo and Dela and is smuggled between worlds by a variety of criminal gangs. Jornan has been known to work alongside the Red Ring Smugglers to help smuggle the drug between the worlds, though I had thought she was going to try to keep low after the busting of her earlier vampire feeding ring. Then again, Xeeonite psychologists often say that criminals usually return to crime quickly because they have made a habit of it.

I also understand the reference to the Portal. Xeeo and Dela are connected by thousands of Portals that allow individuals from both worlds to travel between them. Most Portals are overseen by the governments of both worlds; however, it is common among criminals to have their own illegal Portals that they use to commit all sorts of crimes. That Jornan and her minions have one— possibly more, as most criminals generally have anywhere from two to as much as fifty, depending on the size of the criminal operation in question—surprises me not in the least.

The reference to the Founder, however, makes no sense to me at all. I do a quick search of the mobile Database files, but find no reference in Jornan's bio of any being named 'the Founder.' Possibly a hitherto unknown partner-in-crime? Unknown.

I glance at Sir Alart and whisper, "Founder?"

But Sir Alart shakes his head. "No idea. Keep listening."

I nod as we continue to walk along the catwalk. As it turns out, there is some light in this place; on the floor, near a dozen empty old crates, are portable floodlights that show a sight I had expected to see.

There are at least a dozen dwarves in all, hauling large crates full of super speed in pairs through a larger-than-normal Portal. The Portal appears to be a custom design, possibly made by Jornan herself, because it does not match any Portal design I know of; however, it may actually be an older, discontinued model, because it has a thick layer of dust over it, as if it has not been cleaned or used in a long time. Bluish-white energy crackles within it as dwarves enter and exit it in an orderly manner that prevents the dwarves entering from bumping into the dwarves leaving. A short wooden ramp allows the dwarves to climb up to or down from the Portal easily. I see no power source, though if my readings are correct, I suspect that this Portal has skyras energy coursing through it.

Standing ten feet from the Portal is Jornan ah Kona herself. I snap a picture of her face and compare it to a picture from the mobile Database files. The two look the same: Pale, almost sickly skin, with blackened, rotted teeth from too much super speed usage. Her hair is stringy and graying already, even though her files indicate she is in her late thirties.

I peer over the side of the catwalk to get a better look at Jornan. Though she is not walking, her body shakes and shivers as she watches her minions move the super speed drugs through the Portal to wherever they are sending them. Another common symptom of super speed over-usage is that the user's body shakes uncontrollably, though I do not take that to mean she is weak. On the contrary, records indicate that Jornan is a master witch, as she has ten rings on all of her fingers, which is five more than the typical Delanian witch or wizard has.

Jornan has her hands on her hips, tapping her foot against the floor impatiently. Her men are clearly moving as fast as they can, but dwarves, due to their height and weight, cannot move very fast. That is good news for us, because it will be that much easier for the Knights and I to capture these criminals once we begin the attack.

"By Waran-Una's name, you dwarves have to be the slowest dwarves I've ever had the displeasure of working with," Jornan snaps. She points sharply at the Portal. "Go faster, faster, faster, or do you think you can just take it nice and easy, as if we *don't* have a deadline to meet? If we don't get all of this super speed delivered on time, none of us get paid a cent. Do you hear me? Not one cent."

ALLIANCE

None of Jornan's dwarves respond, but I suspect it's less to do with not having anything to say and more having to do with their fear of her. Mobile Database records indicate, based on the confessions of her arrested ex-partners, that she does not take well to minions who talk back to or disagree with her.

But then one of the dwarves unexpectedly puts down the crate he was lifting and turns to face Jornan. His partner, who lifts the backside of the crate, stares at him in shock and says, with a thick dwarfish accent that even my universal translator has a hard time deciphering, "Rok, what are you doing? Do you expect me to lift this damn crate myself?"

"No," says the dwarf named Rok, shaking his head. He looks at Jornan and folds his arms over his chest. "I'm just sick of Jornan bossing us around like this. You're treating us like pebbles, even though we're working our hardest."

"Do you think I care?" says Jornan in exasperation. "Or do you not realize that we have a strict deadline to meet?"

"I just think I'm tired of working for you," says Rok. He begins listing his grievances off his fingers. "First, you're demanding and unappreciative of our hard work. Second, you never pay us well enough to put up with your crap. And third—"

Jornan raises her right hand before Rok can finish complaining and the ring on her middle finger glows red. While I am not a Delanian witch or wizard myself, I have done enough research to know that a glowing skyras ring means that it is in use.

As soon as the ring finishes glowing, Rok stops speaking. He stares blankly at nothing for a few seconds, as if something has caught his attention. I look to see what he's staring at, but I see nothing but the floor.

Then Rok begins to hyperventilate and back up. He is so terrified by whatever he sees that he trips over his own feet and falls on his behind, but he keeps crawling away even then. I still see nothing coming after him; his fellow dwarves are simply staring at him in confusion, while Jornan watches with an amused expression on her face.

Then Rok begins screaming, "Get away from me, you beast! Get away, or I'll—"

He doesn't finish his sentence because he then curls into a ball and begins sobbing and kicking at whatever he thinks he sees. He grabs at his long beard and pulls at it, screaming something almost incomprehensible about how the thing wants his beard. One of his fellow dwarves looks away in disgust, but the others continue to watch and stare as if this was the most horrifying thing they have seen in their lives.

I feel no horror at this sight, but I notice Sir Alart's heart rate increase and his sweat going down his temple. I know enough about Sir Alart to know that he dislikes criminals, but apparently he has enough empathy left in him to feel disgusted by this display of horror.

The spectacle is over as quickly as it began. Rok now lays on the floor, panting like he has run ten miles in a minute, while his fellow dwarves stand around and look at each other uneasily, none of them making eye contact with their fallen friend.

Jornan, on the other hand, appears to be the only organic being in the warehouse to be entirely unaffected by Rok's morbid display of fear. Mobile Database records indicate that Jornan has a severe lack of empathy, indicating possible sociopathy, though

Xeeonite criminal psychologists disagree.

"What are you idiots staring at?" Jornan snaps at her other minions, who start when they hear her voice. "Get back to work. Rok will be all right in a few minutes. He just needs to take some time to remember why *I'm* the boss and *he* isn't."

Her other minions do not even hesitate to resume working. In fact, they work harder and more efficiently than before, hauling their crates into the Portal quicker than they did earlier. I have never thought that fear to be a great motivator before, but perhaps that is another thing about organic beings that I don't understand.

Then Alart nudges me and I look at him. He holds his communicator up and says, "Think it's time to attack?"

I nod. "Yes. We will take advantage of Jornan having taken out one of her own men for us. It should make it easier for us to defeat the rest."

"All right," said Alart. He raises his communicator up to his mouth and speaks into it, but in a very low tone so neither Jornan nor her minions below can hear us. "Everyone in position, attack now."

We wait for a response from everyone; however, there is no answer, not even from one of the Knights. That is odd. The plan is for everyone to attack as soon as Alart orders them to. That no one responds at all makes no sense.

"Men?" Alart repeats into the communicator, the worry in his voice rising with the tension in his body. "Sir Yaron? Sir Gako? Is anyone there? Hello? Lady Waya?"

Again, there is no response. The communicator is as silent as if it has been turned off, but I know it is active because the green glowing light that signals its activation is on.

Alart looks at me in worry. "What's going on? J997, do you know what the problem is?"

"Without access to their specific communicators, I cannot say for certain what the problem is," I explain in a low whisper. "Did you make sure that everyone's communicator was on?"

"I did," says Alart in annoyance. "I double-checked to make sure that everyone had their communicators on. And yes, before you ask, I made sure they all knew how to use them as well."

"I will try connecting with them," I say. "I know the frequency their radios are tuned to, which is a frequency I have access to."

I go silent, concentrating on connecting to the Knights. Searching ... searching ... searching ... connection fails.

"Hmm," I say. "Perhaps there is something in this warehouse that is blocking radio signals. It is likely magical, whatever it is, because you Delanians rarely use technology to achieve these kinds of feats."

"Does that mean we're on our own?" says Sir Alart. He swears. "Let's retreat. Head back out onto the roof and try to contact everyone again. Maybe the roof is somehow blocking the signal. We can do that because no one even knows we're here yet, so we technically still have the element of surprise on our—"

He is cut off when the catwalk we are on shakes under our feet. We both grab the bars, but it is useless because in the next moment, the catwalk falls out from under our feet. Sir Alart falls, but I try to activate the jets in my feet to keep afloat, although as Sir Alart falls he grabs onto my ankles and we both fall to the floor below.

Sir Alart hits the floor before I do, and I land on top of him.

Sir Alart groans under me, while I look around in time to see Jornan's dwarves surround us, drawing out their weapons; small battle hammers, double-bladed axes, and bronze knuckles. None of those weapons are very high-tech; however, there are enough of those dwarves surrounding us that they do not need high-tech weapons to kill us.

Sir Alart and I scramble to our feet, drawing our own weapons out to defend ourselves, even though I run the numbers and realize that we cannot defeat them all on our own. We stand back-to-back, carefully watching the growling and angry-looking dwarves who look more than ready to kill us.

Jornan walks up at that moment, just outside of the dwarf circle, holding up one of her rings, a blue one, which glows softly in the dark warehouse.

"Did you two honestly believe I didn't expect you Knights to try to track me down?" asks Jornan in an amused voice. "Or that I wouldn't ruin your surprise by using one of my rings to make the catwalk fall apart under you? I'm not that much of an idiot, though I will admit that I didn't expect you to have brought along one of those stupid J bots from Xeeo with you."

"Did you also block off our communicators?" asks Sir Alart, brandishing his silver-white sword at the dwarves, though it only drives them back temporarily, because they then return to their original positions, looking angrier than ever.

"That I did, Sir Knight," says Jornan as she stops just outside of our circle of dwarves. She raises all ten of her rings and flexes her fingers. "It was a simple task, casting a spell that blocks all communication between here and the outside, but sometimes the simplest spells are the best, wouldn't you say?"

"Miss Jornan, you are still under arrest," I respond, resting my finger on the trigger of my PRB. "You and every dwarf here are under arrest for the illegal possession and smuggling of super speed drugs."

"J997, is that really what we should be focusing on at the moment?" asks Sir Alart. "Not, you know, figuring out how to survive against these criminals when we're so badly outnumbered?"

"Your Knight friend has a good point," says Jornan. "We know that we are all going to jail if we get caught. That's why I am going to have my men here take you two apart piece by piece."

She gestures at her dwarves and snaps, "What are you idiots standing around wasting time for? Kill these two and make it quick. We don't have time to waste killing these fools, as fun as it would be to drag out their deaths."

Chapter 2

The dwarves move in on us, swinging their weapons with the ferocity of a barbarian horde. I fire my PRB at one, which knocks him out, while Sir Alart swipes at another criminal with his sword, knocking that dwarf's battle hammer out of his hands and causing the criminal to curse in Dwarfish, though I pay no attention to it because of the other dwarves still moving toward us.

I aim my PRB again and fire, but the dwarves must have seen what happened to their comrade earlier, because they scatter before my laser can hit them. One of the dwarves jumps at me from the side, swinging his ax at me, but I dodge it by stepping aside, allowing the dwarf to smash his ax against the stone floor.

But then another dwarf swings his hammer at me, striking me in the shins. I feel no pain, but the force of the blow does knock me off-balance, forcing me to swing my arms through the air in order to regain my balance. This leaves me open to attack from his allies, who move in with their hammers and axes, yelling and screaming obscenities at me in Dwarfish, but I choose not to translate them because that would distract me unnecessarily.

I stagger backwards out of their reach, their weapons missing me by mere inches. I take aim with my PRB again, but then my sensors pick up another dwarf coming at me from the right. Before I can turn to stop him, his ax comes flying at my hands and knocks my PRB out of them, sending it skittering across the floor out of my reach before another dwarf steps on it with his foot, smashing it in half and effectively making it useless.

Two more dwarves come at me, one from behind and another from the front, but they are under the mistaken belief that because I am unarmed, I am no longer dangerous. I am about to prove them wrong.

I tap my chest, sending a signal through my body. An electrical barrier erupts from my form about three feet on every side. The barrier is a defense mechanism all J bots have, one we rarely use, but when we need it, it's always there and always useful.

The dwarves who come at me run into the barrier and get electrocuted. They scream in pain and fall to the ground, while the other dwarves stand back to avoid suffering the same fate as their comrades. They look like they want to run, because they clearly have no way to deal with my barrier, but they also don't want to suffer Jornan's wrath (though I do not see Jornan anywhere, oddly enough).

Then the dwarves run around me. I turn around and see that they are running toward Sir Alart, who I had almost forgotten about during the struggle. He is fighting two dwarves at once, using his sword to block their hammers and axes. His sword glows, probably from the skyras energy flowing through, because

I see a cord running from his metalligick armor to the handle of his blade.

But as good a fighter as Sir Alart may have been, he is outnumber by the remaining dwarves. I see their plan now. They know they can't touch me while I use this barrier, so they are going after Sir Alart, who they can touch, instead.

Because we are allies, I cannot allow the dwarves to murder Sir Alart. I drop the barrier and point my fingers at the dwarves rushing to kill him. I unleash electric bolts from my fingertips, which strike the dwarves in the backs and cause them all to fall to the floor, stunned by the attack.

"Thanks!" Sir Alart shouts my way as he continues to fight the remaining dwarves. "Now are you just going to stand there or are you going to come and help me?"

I take a step forward to help, but then my sensors warn me of a sudden spike in skyras energy behind me. I jump to the side, avoiding a rock spire that bursts through the floor where I stood, which sends up bits of wood and stone through the air. The spire would have impaled me if I had not moved, though I do not know where it comes from until I look and see Jornan standing on top of one of the nearby crates, her rings glowing on her fingers.

"Lucky," Jornan sneers, raising her hands above her head as energy crackled from her rings. "But you won't be so lucky when I fry you like a fish."

Once again, her skyras levels spike, this time almost going off the charts. A moment later, lightning bolts fire from her rings, thundering through the air toward me.

As quickly as I can, I tap my chest again and my electrical barrier roars to life once more. As soon as it does, the lightning bolts collide with the barrier.

Warning! Barrier rapidly draining power supply. Switching to power-saving—

Denied! Divert full power into maintaining barrier against attack. Automatic switch to power-saving overridden.

Affirmative. Rerouting full power into barrier.

But even as I do that, Jornan's lightning bolts grow stronger and stronger, striking against my barrier with more force than I expected. Even diverting my full power into the barrier is barely enough. Xeeon crystal rapidly draining. Currently at 51%, but is unlikely to stay at that level for long.

Must think of some way to stop Jornan's assault. Almost impossible. With full power diverted to barrier, thought processor is slower than normal. Power at 42%. Still dropping. And fast.

Quickly search Jornan's files in mobile Database. Search for weaknesses. Files claim most of Jornan's magical abilities unknown. Not helpful.

Power overload imminent. Thirty-two percent. Sending message to Database. Error! No connection to Database in Dela. Cannot communicate with Knights outside of warehouse.

"Die, you stupid clicker!" Jornan yells, her voice loud enough that I can hear it even over the sound of her lightning bolts striking my barrier. "Take this!"

Warning! Barrier about to go down! Barrier—

A loud shattering noise, like a glass window breaking, erupts in my audio receptors and I find myself flying. Limbs unresponsive, I fly through one of the windows of the warehouse and crash into the street outside.

The sudden impact against the ground scrambles my senses. I

do a quick scan to ensure that all of my systems are still in operating order, but discover that my power level is now at 22% and my left leg is inoperable. Power level falling fast.

I look around my surroundings and see the warehouse before me and the warehouse behind me. Audio receptors pick up sounds of Sir Alart still battling the Smugglers inside, while Jornan's laughter—louder than normal—can be heard above the crackling of her lightning bolts.

I struggle to rise to my feet in order to help, but my damaged left leg makes that impossible. I nonetheless manage a sitting position, but am unable to make repairs due to a lack of proper tools. Systems scan suggests leg is broken at the knee, which is useless information for me to know because I cannot repair it myself at the moment.

Need to find other Knights and inform them of Jornan's attack. Am puzzled that apparently none of them hear the sounds of battle within. Perhaps Jornan has cast a silencing spell around the warehouse's perimeter as well? Worth investigating later.

I grab onto a nearby crate and use it to help me stand, but I am unable to walk because my left leg is still broken. Nor can I fly, because flying with only one leg is too dangerous. Require a walking stick of some sort for me to lean on while I walk, but scanners show that there is nothing I can use within my immediate vicinity to do that.

Therefore, I lean against the wall of the warehouse, which will have to do for now until I can get my leg repaired or find a suitable stick to help me stand. I hop along on my one good foot, my other leg dangling uselessly behind me, while listening to the sounds of battle raging within the warehouse.

But my progress is slow, despite my efforts. The street is rough and uneven, with trash littered across it. It reminds me of Xeeon back home, although Ra-Dela has noticeably less litter than my home city does. Perhaps there is a reason for that.

In any case, I hop along as fast as I can, hoping I can find the other Knights quickly enough to inform them of this recent turn of events. While I cannot guarantee Sir Alart's survival anymore, I can at least ensure that we arrest a few of Jornan's dwarves, perhaps even Jornan herself if we are fast enough.

That is when I notice someone in metalligick armor lying on the ground not far from me. It appears to be one of the other Knights of Se-Dela, which is good, because I did not think I would find one so quickly. All I need to do is tell him about what has happened and then we can use his communicator to tell the rest of the Knights to attack.

"Sir Knight!" I call as I hop along, raising one hand to my mouth to help increase the volume of my voice. "It's me, J997! Our ally, Sir Alart, is on his own against Jornan and her dwarves in that place. Use your communicator to inform the rest of the Knights about this so we can attack together and hopefully save Sir Alart's life."

The Knight does not so much as budge on the ground. He appears to be ignoring me, but something about his stillness makes me think otherwise.

I stop and continue to lean against the warehouse's exterior as I look down on the still Knight. I activate my sensors, with which I scan the Knight to see if I can determine why he is not moving.

According to my sensors, this Knight is dead. His heart is not beating, his lungs have ceased inhaling and exhaling air, and his throat appears to have been slit by some kind of knife, although I am unable to determine what kind of knife was used to kill him.

In addition, I spot his communicator next to him. It has been irreparably crushed into pieces, appearing as if an individual of great weight had stepped on it. I see claw marks in the earth, but they are impossible to identify due to the crashed communicator covering them.

As a machine, I am incapable of feeling the kind of horror that most organic beings feel whenever they find the corpse of a fellow organic. I do, however, note that this Knight's death complicates the mission and also implies that there may be another reason why the other Knights did not come to our aid when Sir Alart and I started the assault.

I scan the Knight's corpse again. This scan shows traces of slime, with flakes of leathery Grand Lizard skin on his neck near the slit. Odd, because Grand Lizards are known only to exist on Xeeo, near the Dead Lands. Yet this evidence would suggest that this Knight was slain by a Grand Lizard, which makes no sense at all.

It is possible that I might be mistaking the traces of Grand Lizard skin with something else, but I doubt it. The Grand Lizard species exists native only on Xeeo, and even on Xeeo, is only found in the Dead Lands near the city of Xeeon. It is even illegal to transport endangered native Xeeonite animal species to Dela, yet now I cannot deny the obvious evidence of a Grand Lizard's involvement in this Knight's death.

As I lean against the wall, a low hissing sound emits from behind me. Mobile Database records immediately match the hiss with that of a Grand Lizard, which makes me turn around to face the creature, but what I see does not make any sense.

Standing two dozen yards away from me is a humanoid Grand Lizard. That is not an exaggeration. It is literally a humanoid creature that heavily resembles a Grand Lizard. Sensors indicate that it is no illusion cast by Jornan, because the creature has two pumping hearts and appears to be breathing.

I run the appearance of this creature against the thousands of images in the mobile Database, but cannot find any match. I have never seen anything like it before. I cannot feel fear, but I do not like not knowing what this creature is. The Database, even the mobile Database, is supposed to provide me with complete information on every species on Dela and Xeeo, but it apparently does not know what this thing is.

My sensors show me that the humanoid Grand Lizard has blood along the tips of its claws. The blood is dried, but I can still tell that it is human blood. It probably belongs to the dead Knight behind me, or perhaps it belongs to one of the other Knights, who I now assume are all dead, likely thanks to this creature.

I jump backwards away from the unknown creature, because logic dictates that trying to fight a member of a hitherto unknown species is illogical and dangerous. Especially when it is clear that this creature likely killed the other Knights even with their metalligick armor to protect them.

The creature, however, does not appear afraid of me. It advances with its head lowered, the hissing noise emitting from its throat like a snake. While I do not know the strength of its bloody claws, as the mobile Database files contain no information on them at all, they look large and sharp enough to cut through my metal skin and circuitry with no problem.

But unfortunately, I cannot move away from it fast enough. With only one leg, I can jump back only a few inches at a time, while the unknown creature covers several times that ground with each step. It looks like I will have to fight if I wish to survive.

I check my power level again. My energy reserves are at 19%, which reason tells me is not enough to fight against this monster. Yet I have no way to recharge, because there are no recharging stations in Dela. I do have a backup, but I doubt it will do me much good against this creature's might.

The creature, on the other hand, does not appear at all worried about fighting me. It does not hesitate to draw closer and closer, hissing and spitting some kind of saliva that melts through the street as it approaches. My sensors conclude that this creature's saliva is a form of acid, which makes it even less likely that I will survive a fight against it.

With only 19% power left, I cannot use my electrical barrier, because the barrier would rapidly deplete my energy reserves to zero. Nor can I use my lightning bolt fingers, because that, too, will drain my reserves fast. Systems indicate that electrical barrier and lightning bolt fingers are both inoperable, anyway, likely as a result of Jornan's lightning attack from earlier.

Therefore, it seems unlikely that I will be able to defend myself at all. If I was still in Xeeo, I could simply transfer my memory data to the Database until a new body could be constructed for me, but right now I cannot do even that much, so I must defend and care for this body no matter the cost.

I can only watch as the unknown creature approaches. While I cannot feel pain, and therefore cannot fear it, I cannot say that I look forward to being torn apart by this beast. If this creature destroys me, then it is unlikely anyone will be able to put me back together, even if by some stroke of luck a J bot mechanic stumbles upon my remains at some point.

But before the creature's claws are within reach of me, a loud whistle sound nearby causes it to look around in surprise. I also try to find the source of the whistling, but my sensors are unable to pick up anything that could point me in its direction. All I sense is a sudden spike in skyras energy; not as powerful as Jornan's, but strong enough to catch my attention.

However, I do not let that spike distract me. Instead, I take advantage of the creature's distraction to hop away again, although I hop away no faster than I did before. The creature, on the other hand, soon notices my attempts to flee and comes at me again, apparently having lost interest in finding out where the whistling noise is coming from.

Then, without warning, someone jumps down from the roof of a nearby building and lands in the street in between me and the creature. The creature snarls and backs up, perhaps taken by surprise by the newcomer's sudden appearance, while I stop hopping long enough to look at the being as she rises to her full height.

Initially, I mistake her for Jornan, because she is a female human wearing witch robes and has skyras rings along her fingers. But then, upon further inspection, I notice that she has only five skyras rings, rather than ten, and she is skinnier than Jornan. Her skin is much paler, too, and she has shorter hair, but I cannot see her face because she is not facing me. All I know is that she has an immense amount of skyras energy flowing through her body and rings, if my scanners are accurately reporting her energy levels, although it is still not quite as much as Jornan's.

"Who are you?" I ask, though the witch does not turn to face me. "Identify yourself."

"Later," says the witch, her voice short and to the point. "Right now, we have to deal with this unnatural beast."

The creature has gotten over its shock at her appearance by now. Still, it does not attack her right away, but instead steps back, its reptilian eyes scanning her like it is trying to size her up. That made the creature far more intelligent than a Grand Lizard, which again makes me wonder exactly what it is.

The witch raises her right hand, which has three skyras rings on it, red, yellow, and blue, and says, "Foul creature, why don't ye crawl back into the pit from which ye came? Be gone!"

Her red ring flares and a hot flame shoots from it like fire from the mouth of a Dead Lands fire spitter. The flame strikes the creature in the neck, causing it to yelp in pain, but that does nothing to put out the fire, which clings to its skin like a parasite. Smoke rises from the spot as the lizard creature bats at the fire in an attempt to put it out, but the fire appears incapable of being put out.

Then the witch's yellow ring flashes and lightning shoots from it. The blast strikes the creature directly in the chest, sending it flying backwards through the air, the flame still affixed to its neck. The creature lands on the street hard and begins rolling around in pain, hissing and growling as the flames spread across its body like fire in a dry forest.

Without warning, the witch whirls around to face me. She has a pointed face, with golden eyes that my mobile Database records say are common among Delanian humans. She strides toward me, saying as she does so, "Come on, ye walking scrap heap! We must flee, and quickly, before the creature's brothers discover it and come after us."

"The creature has brothers?" I say, hopping backwards as I speak. "And why should I trust you? I do not even know your name yet."

"Because I am a friend," says the witch, holding out her hands toward me. "If ye need a name, then call me Palos. But we must go, because ye are clearly injured and in desperate need of medical attention."

"Actually, as a robot, I need a certified technician with experience in J bot design to repair me," I say, as I run the name 'Palos' through the mobile Database, only to discover that the name matches none of the records. "Unless you happen to be one yourself or know how to find one on Dela, I am afraid I will have to turn down your offer of help."

"Stubborn machine," Palos says. "I am your ally, though ye do not know it yet. For I, too, fight against Jornan, though for different reasons than ye."

"You are not in the Database," I say, even though I doubt that sentence means much to her. "Are you a member of the Knights of Se-Dela? Or perhaps, based on your clothing and skyras rings, you belong to the Just Order of Witches and Wizards instead?"

"I belong to an organization of which your 'Database' knows nothing," says Palos, still holding her hands out toward me. "Come with me, I say, unless ye wish to suffer the same fate that befell this poor noble Knight and his comrades."

She gestures at the dead Knight lying on the ground nearby. Considering how she mentions his 'comrades,' I assume that my original theory is correct, that the other Knights have also been killed, likely by that strange humanoid lizard creature.

Before I can respond to her, a familiar hissing noise behind my back forces me to look in that direction. Another humanoid lizard creature is walking toward me, though I do not know where it comes from. While its partner continues to hiss and burn to death, this one simply keeps walking forward, as if it is not afraid of either of us.

"There are more of these creatures?" I say, though less out of shock and more out of curiosity. "How odd. The Database has no information on this species at all, but there are apparently at least two members of this species here. This doesn't make any sense at all."

Palos grabs my shoulder and pushes me back behind her. I hobble around on one leg for a moment before losing my balance and falling on my behind with a clatter, though I look up in time to see Palos striding toward the humanoid lizard creature without any trace of fear in her step. That impresses me, because I know that most organic beings would be terrified of fighting these kinds of creatures.

"That's because, machine, these creatures are not natural at all," says Palos without looking at me as her yellow ring flashes with power. "These are native neither to Dela nor Xeeo; therefore, they must be destroyed."

I do not understand what she means by any of that, but I decide to ask her later when the situation is not as tense. Instead, I try to stand back up again while also watching Palos and the lizard creature approaching each other rapidly.

The lizard humanoid looks like it is going to pounce, but then

Palos throws a lightning bolt at it. The lizard humanoid, however, jumps to the side, neatly avoiding her attack, and then rushes at Palos far faster than before. In fact, it dashes so quickly that even my optics have difficulty keeping up with it, to the point where it looks like little more than a green blur now.

Palos does not seem afraid of it. Her red ring glows and she throws up a wall of fire between herself and the lizard humanoid. The lizard humanoid veers to the right just before it runs directly into the wall of fire, which is apparently too wide for it to run around because through the gaps in the wall I see the creature head back the way it came. The lizard humanoid stops about two dozen feet away from the wall of fire and then turns around to face us, but with the fire crackling between us and the creature, it seems unlikely to attack us again. It takes a defensive gesture, crouching low to the ground, although with my knowledge of the lizard humanoid as limited as it is, it may very well have been planning to attack us again for all I know.

"Run, foul creature," says Palos, though I doubt the lizard humanoid can hear her above the roar of the flames, much less understand her words. "Run and do not look back, unless ye want to die a terrible death."

Her words are quite silly to me, but having just seen her kill another one of those lizard humanoids earlier, I am in no mood to offer my opinion on the subject.

Instead, I run a quick check of my power level. By now, it is at 17%, which is surprising, considering how little energy I have consumed. I will definitely need to find a recharge station quickly. Perhaps this Palos woman knows where I can find one in Dela, or maybe the organization she works with has one.

Before I can ask her about that, however, my systems pick up a spike of skyras energy nearby. In fact, according to my scanners, the spike is coming from directly above us, forcing me to look upwards to see what is causing that spike.

A huge ball of water is falling toward us at an alarming speed. I yell at Palos, but she notices it before I finish drawing her attention to it, and thrusts her yellow ring in its direction.

A lightning bolt—bigger than the last few—lances out of Palos's yellow ring and strikes the water sphere dead on. The result: The water sphere explodes with a loud crackling noise, spreading water everywhere and forcing me to cover my head with my arms. The water splashes over me, but I do not feel it, although my sensors inform me that none of the water has soaked into my interior, thankfully enough.

As for Palos, she is dripping wet, and her wall of fire has apparently been extinguished, because I no longer see it standing between us and the lizard humanoid. Instead, there is a wall of steam, but through the steam, I can already see the lizard humanoid dashing toward us again.

Palos notices the lizard humanoid, too, and shoots another lightning bolt at it, but the lizard humanoid dodges by jumping over it. It lands on the ground with ease and continues charging at Palos, now too close for her to attack.

Then I notice her gray ring on her left hand flash and in an instant, Palos is gone. The lizard humanoid stops before it runs into the spot where she stood moments ago. It looks around in puzzlement, a feeling I would have shared with it if I could feel, because I am just as ignorant of what happened to Palos as it is.

Then Palos reappears behind the lizard humanoid and grabs

31

the back of its neck with her right hand. Her red ring flashes and the lizard humanoid bursts into flame before it can even scream. In fact, it does not just burst into flame, but it also burns into ash. Sensors indicate that Palos had superheated the lizard humanoid to over 300 degrees, which is an unusual amount of heat for a Delanian witch to generate. That tells me that Palos is far more dangerous than I originally believed, which means I must keep an eye on her in case she turns out to be hostile to me.

Dropping the ash to the ground, Palos then looks up and says, "I see you, Jornan! Are you going to come down and fight or are you going to—"

Jornan appears behind Palos as silently and abruptly as Palos appeared behind that lizard humanoid. She grabs at Palos, but Palos disappears again and reappears beside me. She raises her ringed fingers above her head, which the mobile Database tells me is a common battle stance for Delanian witches and wizards to take.

Jornan, on the other hand, merely crosses her arms, scowling at us both. She looks the same as she did before, but I notice a cut above her right eye. Perhaps it is a blow Sir Alart landed on her, which is the most likely explanation for it, because it had not been there the last time I saw her.

"Palos of Targia," says Jornan in a mocking tone. "I believe that we've met before, haven't we?"

"I am surprised ye remembered, ye scoundrel," says Palos. I sense her skyras levels rapidly rising, as are Jornan's. "That was ten years ago, at the Tournament of Magic. 'Twas when I uncovered your dastardly scheme to steal the Tournament's Trophy for your own nefarious ends."

"And I would have gotten away with it, too, if you hadn't gotten in my way," says Jornan. "But no matter. What's past is past, and there's no changing it. I would ask why you are here or how you even know I was here, but I have more urgent matters to attend to, so I think I'll just skip to the part where I murder you in cold blood and destroy your little robot friend while I'm at it."

Jornan hurls a lightning bolt at Palos and me. Palos responds by throwing her own lightning bolt at Jornan, even though I am about to tell Palos that that would not be a wise move at all. But I am too late and so can only watch as the two lightning bolts meet halfway between us and Jornan.

When they do, the lightning bolts explode. As soon as they explode, however, Palos bends over and grabs my arm, and then, before I know it, we are gone, although not before I hear Jornan cursing in Delanian above the sound of the exploding lightning bolts.

Chapter 3

What I am experiencing now must be Delanian teleportation. I have never experienced it before. On Xeeon, I have used teleportation pads to go from one end of the city to the other, but this is completely unlike that.

Xeeonite teleportation is gradual, with the environment melting around you like metal left out in the Dead Lands' sun for too long. It is one of the few areas where Delanians have us beat, because teleportation is a highly complex science, one which Xeeonite scientists struggle to understand.

Delanian teleportation, however, is quick. One instant, I am watching the explosion caused by the lightning bolts striking each other and listening to Jornan's angry curses; the next, I am sitting in a dark room that I do not recognize, with Palos standing next to me, her wet hair clinging to her head like a starfish on a rock.

Without waiting for Palos to explain where we are, I immediately begin a scan of the area. The room is square, at 140 square feet, with a few inches to spare in either direction. The ceiling is five feet above our heads, while a closed metal door is the only entrance or exit in this room. Temperature is 70 degrees, although it is slightly warmer near the vents on the ceiling, where air is blowing through, though it does not feel like Xeeonite interior heating. That suggests that this room is in a colder area, though where it might be exactly, I do not know.

But despite knowing all of this information about our destination immediately, I still do not know the name of this room or its exact location. If the Database existed in Dela, I would be able to pinpoint this place's location with exactitude.

Palos lets go of my arm and staggers to the side. Sensors indicate she is far more tired than I first thought. Still, there is nothing I can do to help her, because my inoperable leg has left me unable to do as much, especially with my extremely low power level.

Instead, I ask, "Palos, where did you teleport us to? I do not recognize this room."

Panting, Palos wipes her hair off her forehead and says, "Law enforcer, we are in the only safe spot in the world right now. Not a single soul can find us here. Not even Jornan can find us, even if she uses the blackest magic she knows."

"I am sorry, but that is not very specific," I say. "I need the name and location of this place so I can estimate how far I am from the nearest Portal. I need to return to Xeeo right away so I can report on what happened and receive the repairs I need."

"I apologize, law enforcer, but we cannot let ye do that, at least not right away," says Palos. She puts her hands together, a gesture I sometimes see Delanian humans do when they wish to emphasize their apologies. "We cannot guarantee that ye will be safe. I must speak first with the Head before we let ye go anywhere."

"Who is the Head?" I say. "May I speak with him?"

"Not yet," says Palos, shaking her head. "The Head may not even wish to speak with ye. She—the Head is female, by the way —is a busy person, after all, and rarely makes time to speak with non-members such as yourself unless it is urgent."

"Non-members?" I repeat. "I still do not understand. Are we in your organization's headquarters? Just what *is* your organization? Can you at least tell me the name so I may catalog it in the mobile Database?"

"Nay," says Palos. "Ye are not even supposed to be here, law enforcer, but I hope that the Head will understand that I had no choice but to bring ye here."

Before I can respond to that, the door I noticed earlier bursts open. Two beings enter the room, two beings who I have never seen before in my life and for whom the mobile Database records fail to provide any information.

The first one is a dwarf, but unlike most dwarves, he is completely bald, without any hair on his head or his face. He wears thick wizard robes, like the kind the mobile Database tells me are worn by wizards living in the Winterlands, but I see no skyras rings on his fingers, which makes me wonder why he wears that clothing. Sensors indicate that his blood pressure is rising, which tells me that he is angry, though I do not know what he is angry about.

The second is a female elf, one with short blonde hair. She is wearing a simple Delanian tunic, though she has apparently sewn pockets into it, or perhaps someone else sewed pockets onto it, based on its appearance. In addition, the tunic is made of a thick wool, which suggests she has been in a cold environment recently. Unlike her dwarfish friend, she is armed with a sword, although it looks different from the skyras swords usually used by the Knights of Se-Dela, as it is a dead gray color rather than a shining white. And unlike her friend, she is not angry, but she is worried, perhaps dreading some future problem that is going to happen.

Palos turns from me to face the two newcomers, saying as she does so, "Ah, Rozan, Nacina, I—"

"Don't say another word," the dwarf snaps, pointing at her with an accusatory finger. "You know the rules, but you went against them anyway."

"Rozan, there's no need for that tone," says the female elf, who I assume must be Nacina, in a much lower tone than the dwarf. She puts one calming hand on his shoulder. "I'm sure that Palos has a reason for her actions. Right, Palos?"

"Of course I do," says Palos, folding her arms across her chest. "I will explain them directly to the Head herself if I must. Let it be known that I did not save this machine to spite our organization."

"I don't care what your reasons are for saving it," says Rozan, shrugging off Nacina's hand and pointing at me as if I can not understand what he is saying. "The rules say that we're not supposed to have any non-members of the Foundation inside either of our bases. And this robot is certainly not a member of the Foundation, for sure."

I quickly run the term 'Foundation' through the mobile Database files. My search turns up the Foundation for Homeless Jikorian Children, a non-profit Xeeonite charity that helps get homeless Jikorian children off the streets, but I sincerely doubt that that Foundation is the same as this Foundation, not in the least because the mobile Database files show that the charity does not have a Delanian branch.

"I am quite aware of the rules, Rozan, but I still refuse to apologize for my decision," says Palos. She gestures at me. "After all, if I had not saved him, then Jornan would have destroyed him. Would that have been a good thing? Of course not."

"You're acting like this robot is valuable," says Rozan. He glares at me. "All I see is trouble. Now that he's here, he knows we exist, and no one is supposed to know we exist. Not even Waran-Una knows we exist, for the earth's sake."

"I think we should discuss this another time," says Nacina, before Palos can respond. "Palos, you need to report to the Head about the status of your mission, although I can see that it clearly did not go as planned if you had to return without stopping Jornan."

"Yea, I did fail to stop her," says Palos with a sigh. "Jornan proved far smarter than I thought. She killed all of the Knights and has already moved most of the cargo to Xeeo."

"Damn it," says Rozan. "I should have come with you. Jornan wouldn't have stood a chance against me. Would have been running like the coward she is, she would have."

"Excuse me," I say, causing all three of the Foundation members to look at me. "I still do not know what is going on here. Does anyone care to explain?"

"No," says Rozan. He shakes his head at me. "Don't try to trick us, you robot. We're not telling you a thing about us until the Head gives us permission to. Until then, keep your mouth shut."

His rudeness does not phase me, although I am disappointed that I will not be learning about the true nature of this organization anytime soon, or so it seems.

Therefore, I ask, "All right. But if you will not tell me that, then will you at least take me to a certified J bot technician and a certified recharging station as well? My left leg is broken, you see, and I am extremely low on power as well."

I say this while pointing at my leg, which is still inoperable. I also do a quick check of my power level: 15%. It is draining far more rapidly than I thought, which makes me hope that these Foundation members will at least grant me that request, if nothing else.

"Don't know if we can do even that much," says Rozan. He looks at Nacina. "Do we even have a technician around here? Or a recharge station?"

"I don't know," says Nacina with a shrug. "I tend to doubt it, but you never know. And we could always use magic to repair him, if necessary."

That thought makes me uneasy. Delanian magic rarely interacts well with Xeeonite technology, even though both use skyras energy. While I know that there are some individuals on both Dela and Xeeo whom are studying ways to connect the two, there is a good reason they are usually kept separate. I remember one time seeing a visiting Delanian wizard attempt to put back together a fallen comrade of mine, which ended with my comrade bursting into flame. It might be better for me to wait until I can return to Xeeo before getting the help I need.

"Robot, you stay here until we return," says Rozan, pointing at me as if he thinks I am going to try to run away. "We are going to speak with the Head about you first. But don't worry; we won't be long at all, although if things go the way I think they will, then I doubt you'll like it."

Rozan then turns and stomps out of the room, followed by Nacina, who looks back at me apologetically, and then Palos, who does not say another word to me as she leaves. I watch all three of them go until they close the door behind themselves, leaving me alone in this strange room.

My internal clock shows that thirty minutes pass before the door opens again. While I am incapable of sleeping, I do go into power conservation mode while I wait, as my power level is too low for me to risk waiting in full-power mode. This turns off some of my functions, such as my connection with the Database, but that is fine because I do not need it at the moment.

When the door opens, however, I raise my head in time to see a man enter the room, a man I have never seen before. He is tall and thin, similar to Jornan, but his face is scarred, like he was attacked by a wild animal at some point.

He carries at his side a large black toolbox, which he rests on the floor near my broken leg. He gets on his knees, flips open the lid of his toolbox, and begins digging through it for the tools he needs.

"Excuse me," I say, raising a hand in an attempt to catch his attention. "Who are you? Are you going to repair my broken leg?"

The man does not answer. He simply glances at me before returning to digging through his toolbox. Sensors indicate that he is not afraid of me and his vocal chords are in working order. For whatever reason, he simply sees no reason to speak with me.

I do not like having people operate on me who I know nothing about, so I ask, "Are you a certified J bot technician? If so, may I see your certification? All certified technicians have one, you know."

The man still does not answer. He does not even show me his certification, which makes me uneasy. Protocol states that only certified J bot technicians are allowed to make repairs or modifications to J Series Robotic Law Enforcers. This is due to our unique designs and specifications, which require years of training to understand, which is why most generic robotics technicians are not allowed to work on us.

That this man refuses to show me his certificate, if indeed he has one at all, is a warning sign. If we were still in Xeeo, I would have sent out an alarm to the other J bots informing them of this man's illegal activity and he would be behind bars before sundown. While illegally operating on a J bot is not the most serious crime in the world, it is still serious enough to earn a criminal several years in jail if caught in the act.

This man, probably a Delanian, clearly needs to be told about this. Not only that, but I will need to arrest him as well and bring him before the Court of Xeeo to have his fate decided.

As I think all of this, the man pulls out a portable x-ray device. He waves it over my leg, probably to find out exactly what the problem is, and observes what it shows on the screen, although I cannot see it myself due to my current position.

So I say to the man, "Sir, if you are not a certified J bot technician, then I will have to arrest you and take you to the Court of Xeeo. Illegally operating on a J bot without a license is a criminal offense punishable by up to ten years in prison."

The man does not so much as glance at me. He simply removes the x-ray device from my leg and resumes digging through his toolbox, perhaps looking for the best tool to fix my leg.

I do not like the fact that he ignores me, though I am not surprised. I have run into this kind of criminal before, the kind who freely breaks the law and does not show any remorse or regret over it, even when you explain to him in the plainest language that his actions are criminal. I always find that attitude in career criminals, which makes me believe that this man must be used to breaking the law, although the mobile Database does not show any records on any men who resemble this one.

But I do not know how I am supposed to arrest him. My power level is too low for me to try to fight him, not to mention my leg is still broken. I do not even have my PRB anymore, which I left back at the scene of Jornan's crime. I can try to use my lightning bolt fingers, but that might drain too much of my power too quickly.

It appears, then, that I have no choice but to wait for this man to finish operating on me. As he does not appear to have a certificate that allows him to operate on J bots, I can only guess at the damage he will cause as he attempts to repair my leg. It will probably be quite extensive, as untrained technicians usually make many mistakes when they attempt to repair a J bot.

"J997's the identification number, right?" says the man, looking at me with a hard eye.

"Yes," I say without hesitation. "And I will have you know that what you are about to do is highly illegal. If you stop now, before you try to work on my leg, I will not bring criminal charges against you."

"Right, well, if I'm going to be working on you, I'm gonna need to knock you out for a bit," says the man. He lifts a tiny remote control. "This is a robot nullifier. It can shut off any robot I want for as long as I want. Don't worry, though, it won't cause you any lasting or permanent damage."

"Usage of robot nullifiers on J bot law officials was banned by the Law Enforcement Aid Act of 3025," I say. "By using that on me, you are adding another twenty years to your ten year sentence for your crime of operating on me without a certificate."

"Sure," says the man, nodding. "But you know, the only reason I'm telling you this is because I have great respect for you J bots and I think you deserve to know what's going to happen to you before it happens."

"If you had true respect for us, you would not be doing this to me at all," I say. "It is illogical to claim to respect us while simultaneously breaking the very law we are sworn to protect."

"Let's agree to disagree," says the man. "Good night."

He presses a button on the nullifier before I can do anything else. My message alert center immediately shows me that all of my systems are shutting down fast, so fast that I—

Chapter 4

SYSTEM REBOOTING. SCANNING FOR DAMAGE ... SCANNING .... CONGRATULATIONS! NO DAMAGE FOUND ON J ROBOT LAW ENFORCER J997. J997 FULLY OPERATIONAL. POWER LEVEL AT 90%. PROCEED TO FULLY BOOT ALL SYSTEMS.

The ceiling gradually comes into view as my vision clears. While J bots have some of the most advanced computer systems on Xeeo, it still takes a little time for us to fully reboot if our systems are knocked offline. My scanners report that my body is fine, however, which makes me glad, because interior damage is difficult to fix without a certified technician to help.

My memory, however, takes slightly longer to fully restore. Soon, however, I remember that it is that mysterious man who had knocked me out—the untrained technician who thinks he can repair me as easily as any other robot.

But according to my scanners, my body is in one piece. There are no problems anywhere. Everything is in perfect condition. Even my power levels are high again, which tells me that the

Foundation members must have recharged my power somehow.

As for my surroundings, I am still in that same room that I was in before, the average, featureless room with a single door. I am alone in this room, but that does not bother me because sensors indicate that I can bend my left knee and move my left leg again. Not only that, but sensors also indicate that my left leg moves even better than it did before it broke.

While what that man did before was clearly illegal, I cannot deny that he does a good job, an even better job than what many other certified technicians who have worked on me have done. Maybe he really does have a certificate; at least he knows what he is doing, anyway.

Despite his good work, I will still have to bring him in. Now that my power has returned, and my leg is movable again, it will be much easier to catch and apprehend him, although first I must find out where I am and what is going on. Upholding the law is of utmost importance, but it is far more urgent at the moment that I find out where I am and how I got here.

I try to sit up, only to discover that my movement is limited. I look down at my arms, legs, and chest and see that they are strapped down by thick leather straps. Sensors indicate that these straps are not normal straps, but are in fact made of dwarfish leather, the strongest type of leather in both Dela and Xeeo, and nearly impossible for most beings to break.

I understand now. The Foundation must have strapped me down to the floor when that mysterious man worked on me earlier. Considering how Rozan distrust me, I am not surprised to see that they went to great lengths to keep me down in one place. They must not think I am too much of a threat, however, because

45

I am still functioning without any problems.

I am barely disturbed by this development, however. While dwarfish leather is a strong substance, we J bots can lift up to 500 pounds of weight. Our strength is unparalleled in many cases; therefore, I doubt it will take much of my strength to free myself from this simple trap.

I strain against the straps, which hold tight against my resistance. These must be new because they barely budge against my efforts, but even new leather can be broken with enough effort, so I keep trying. Sooner or later, I will break free, because unlike organic beings, I do not tire at all.

But despite putting all of my effort into straining against these straps, they seem to be getting tighter, not lighter. This makes no sense at all, because that would imply that these straps are somehow aware that I am trying to break free. They are simply inanimate objects. Perhaps they are magically enchanted to become tighter if met with resistance, a common tactic I have heard certain Delanian witches and wizards do. Unfortunately, my sensors cannot tell for sure.

Whatever the case, I will not give up that easily. All I need to do is use my laser vision—a feature that all J bots have, although one I do not use regularly due to its dangerous nature—to cut through the straps. While dwarfish leather may be the strongest leather in the two worlds, that does not mean it can survive a laser.

Twin lasers, red in color, shoot from my optics and strike the straps holding down my body to the ground. As I predicted, the straps snap instantly, allowing me to sit up and move my limbs freely. While I cannot get cramped arms or legs like organic beings can, I do prefer having the freedom to move my limbs, because it means I can find out where I am and how I got here.

I stand up, dusting off my body. I twist and turn my left leg to assure myself one last time that it does indeed still work, and then step forward with it. When I do not fall forward on my face, I walk up to the door, thinking that this is much easier than I originally thought. I find it strange how the Foundation members leave me unguarded, but perhaps the door is locked.

I analyze the door and discover that, unlike most of the doors back on Xeeo, this one does not slide open. I am reminded again that I am in Dela, a technologically primitive world in comparison to Xeeo, but this is not a problem. I know how to operate Delanian doors, so I reach for the doorknob.

That is when the leather straps from before wrap around my legs and pull. Taken by surprise, I fall to the floor as the straps try to drag me back to my original position, but I am not stunned by this fall. Instead, I twist my head over my shoulder to gain a better understanding of what is happening.

The leather straps that I split earlier are much longer now than they once were. They move like snakes, wrapped so tightly around my legs that I do not see any way I can force them off.

My logical mind wonders how this is even possible. I did not detect any skyras energy channeling through them earlier. This is clearly an example of Delanian magic at work, however, which makes me wonder how I missed it. Maybe Delanian magic is far subtler than I can detect with my sensors.

In any case, I do not intend to be held down again. I fire another set of lasers at the straps, cutting through them again. Now that my legs are free again, I stand up and back up toward the door, while the straps hover toward me again. I see no reason why they should, as I have already cut them down to size twice. Analysis suggests that Delanian magic is responsible for their increasing length, although that does not explain exactly how it works. Perhaps the extra length is hidden under the floor

In any case, it does not matter how it works, because the straps are coming at me and do not seem likely to give up anytime soon. Considering how ineffective my lasers have proven against them, I conclude that the only way out of this situation is to escape from this room.

I turn around and reach for the doorknob, but before I can grab it, the door opens and I find myself face-to-face with a Delanian human who I do not recognize. He is a bulky human, with five skyras rings on his fingers. He looks like the sort of human who does well as a guard.

"What?" says the man, who has a deep voice. "What's going on in here? How did you escape the—"

I do not wait for him to finish. Instead, I punch him in the gut, which causes him to gasp in pain, and follow it up by jolting him with electricity. The electric jolt causes him to collapse to the floor, allowing me to jump over him as the straps continue to reach for me.

Landing on the floor, I turn around and fire my eye lasers at the straps again. The lasers cut through the straps and cause them to shrink back, perhaps afraid, although I do not know because I kick the unconscious man into the room and slam the door closed behind him afterward. I hear the straps beating against the door, but it is clear that they are not strong enough to break it down and are therefore not going to be a threat to me anytime soon.

Shaking my head, I look around at my surroundings. It appears I am standing inside the hallway of a castle. The walls, floor, and ceiling are all cobblestone and sensors indicate that they are normally very cold. Sensors also show that the hallway is warmed by some kind of external heat source, but I am unable to locate it. It is probably magic, but at the moment I do not need to confirm that. Instead, I need to find out where I am and how to get out of here and reconnect with the Database.

Just as I come to that decision, a voice shouts, "Hey, what are you doing out here? You're not supposed to be out!"

I look in the direction of that voice and see two elves running toward me. Neither of them have skyras rings, but they are holding staffs and swords. Old-fashioned weaponry, in other words, that will be completely ineffective against my abilities.

I raise my hand to unleash finger lightning bolts at the elves, but one of the elves vanishes before I can do so. My scanners search the hall for the missing elf, but I cannot find him anywhere, although his friend is still running at me and is almost within range of hitting me with his weapon.

So I fire my finger lightning bolts, but the elf jumps over them and lands in front of me. He swings his staff at my head, which I catch with no issue.

"That was a pathetic move on your part," I say, holding back his staff with ease. "I can sense that you are trying your best, but I am afraid your best is not enough."

Oddly, the elf smirks. "Get 'im, Garga!"

I have no idea who 'Garga' is until I hear something whistling through the air at me.

Before I can identify the source of that whistling, something thick and solid slams into the left side of my head. The blow—while not painful, as I cannot feel pain—completely disrupts my sensors and sends me staggering to the left, letting go of the first elf's staff as I do so.

WARNING! Damage to optics extensive. Activating auto-repair features.

I shake my head, however, because I have no time to let my auto-repair features work. These two elves require my fullest attention, so I must put deactivate the auto-repair features until I can find a more convenient time to use them.

Besides, my optics appear to be working fine because I can see the two elves surrounding me, holding their staffs before them like they intend to beat me to a pulp with them. Still, my vision is not entirely clear; my left optic is choppy, forcing me to rely on my right optic more than I usually do.

"Stupid machine," says the first elf. "We saw you assault the guard. We're not going to let you walk without first getting permission from the Head, which we know you don't have, so don't even pretend that you do."

"I never would have pretended," I say. "After all, we J bots are incapable of lying or deception. All I want to know is where I am and how to get out of here."

"Not until the Head says so," says the second elf, the one named Garga, who has a higher voice than his friend. "Until then, you have to stay where you're supposed to: In that little room, strapped like a rat."

These two elves clearly believe they can defeat me, but they just as clearly do not know the full extent of my powers and abilities. They may be able to dodge my finger lightning bolts, but finger lightning bolts are not the only tricks up my sleeve.

I tap my chest, causing an electrical barrier to extend three feet from my body. The barrier strikes the two elves and knocks them out immediately. They fall to the floor, their staffs clattering by their sides, and as soon as they do, I deactivate my electrical barrier. The two elves' bodies smoke slightly from being burnt by my electricity, but scanners indicate that they are still alive, albeit unlikely to awake anytime soon.

But even though they are both out cold, that does not solve my problem, because I still do not know where I am. I doubt, however, I will get much of an opportunity to find out, because if these two know I am here, then it is highly likely that the rest of the Foundation knows of my escape as well.

Which way should I go? I do not know because I do not have any information or even a map on the general layout of this place. Nor can I rely on satellites in orbit to provide me with any information, because Dela does not have any artificial satellites, much less artificial satellites connected to the Database.

Standard protocol for J bots in this type of situation is to head in the direction of Xeeon, where the Database is kept. Unfortunately, I cannot even follow standard protocol in this situation because of the lack of connection to the Database on Dela, which does not even exist here.

What I need is information, and quickly. These two elves, obviously agents of the Foundation, will likely be able to tell me what I need to know, but I must interrogate them quickly, because I do not know how long I have until other Foundation agents come by to check up on me.

I kneel over the elf known as Garga. His eyes are rolled into the back of his head, but I slap him across the face in an effort to awaken him quickly.

It works, because Garga shakes his head and says, "What the —" before I put a hand over his mouth and tighten my grip.

"Do not try to scream," I say, keeping my audio level low to avoid awaking his ally, while also pinning Garga to the floor with my knee. "Or teleport. I only want information on this place. Is that understandable?"

Garga glares at me, which tells me that I need to be more explicit in my request.

"Listen here," I say, leaning a little closer in, an intimidation technique I learned over my years of interrogating captured criminals. "If you do not answer my questions about the Foundation, I will do far worse to you than simply electrocute you. Do you understand?"

He keeps glaring at me, but he does nod slightly. I notice him reaching for his staff, so I fire my lasers at his staff before he can so much as touch it. The laser knocks his staff out of his reach, causing him to curse, although his curse is unintelligible due to my hand covering his mouth.

"I suggest you do not try and attack me while I am not looking," I say. "Because that will end quite badly for you, I promise."

Garga still does not look happy, but he has no more weapons to reach for, so I say, "Now, will you cooperate or will you not?"

My facial recognition technology says that Garga looks like he would rather kill himself than cooperate with me, but then he nods again. I take my hand off his mouth, but rest it on his throat to keep him pinned so he does not think he can escape.

"Dumb machine," Garga spits at me; quite literally, he spits saliva at me, although I do not care. "Stupid robot. Idiotic clicker."

"I did not ask for you to insult me," I say, "as that is not a good method of cooperation. Instead, I would like to know the location of the nearest exit, as well as the location of the building itself."

"Can't tell you any of that," Garga says. "The Head doesn't want you knowing anything she hasn't approved of you to know."

"I do not care," I say. I tighten my grip around his neck; not enough to choke him, but enough to make him think twice about refusing to tell me what I need to know. "All I wish to know is where I am and how to get out of here. Hardly what I call an unreasonable demand."

"Doesn't matter if your demand is 'unreasonable' or not," says Garga. "What matters is that the Head says you aren't allowed to know, so you aren't allowed to—"

I slap him across the face again. "I do not care. How many times must I say that before you understand it? Must I speak in Elvish Delan before you will understand what I want?"

A trickle of blood appears from the corner of Garga's mouth. I have no intention of beating him senseless, but as a J bot, I am authorized to use force during interrogations in order to gain the intelligence I need. It is sometimes the only way to learn what I need to know, especially in situations like this.

"Perhaps I should make it simpler for you," I say. "Instead of telling me where this place is located, why don't you simply point me in the direction of the nearest exit?"

I fully expect Garga to insult me again, which would require me to become far less gentle and merciful in order to get what I need.

Instead, Garga raises a hand and points a shaky finger to the left end of the hallway. He doesn't meet my eyes as he says, "Just go down that way. You'll find stairs going up to the next floor. Keep following the stairs, and you'll eventually find the exit."

Garga appears to be telling the truth, so I say, "All right. Thank you for your cooperation, Garga. This will be very helpful in my escape. But unfortunately for you, I will have to knock you out for now. Don't worry; it will only be a little while, I promise."

I slap Garga again, this time with far more effort than before. The blow knocks him out and I stand up. His friend has not moved a muscle since I knocked him out as well, which is good because that is one less obstacle I will have to deal with on my way out of this place.

I run toward the left end of the hallway, which appears to be a heavy stone door, although where it leads to I do not know. My guess is that it will open up to a staircase that will lead me upward, as all clues support the theory that I am somewhere underground. It is the only reason why this hallway and the room I was in earlier do not have any windows, although they do have ventilation systems that likely funnel air into these areas to make them breathable to the organic Foundation members who work down here.

When I reach the door, I push it open and enter. I expect to find myself in a narrow stairwell, but instead, I stumble into another room, this one much wider and open than the one I had been kept in like a prisoner.

Like the hallway, this room has cobblestone walls and floors, as well as a ceiling made out of that same material. Glowing candles hang from the ceiling, which appear to be the only sources of light in this room, shining as brightly as the indoor lights of most Xeeonite buildings.

These candles show me a dozen beings—probably Foundation agents, although due to their lack of identification I do not know for certain—sitting around a table talking amongst themselves. On the table itself are maps, skyras rings, and pictures, which tells me that these agents are probably discussing Foundation plans, whatever those are.

But if that is what they are talking about, they are no longer doing so, because now every eye in the room is on me. Many of them look at me in surprise, as if they had not expected me to enter, but none of them move to get up and try to grab me.

I turn to leave, but when I try to pull open the door, I find that it refuses to budge. That is odd, because I opened it just fine before. Brief analysis shows no reason for this, except that this door appears to have been locked by skyras, although the traces of skyras on the door are very faint and barely noticeable.

Whatever the reason for this mystery, it is not good. That means that I am now locked in this room with these beings who may wish to harm me.

"J997?" says a voice behind me, one I recall from earlier, as it sounds exactly like the voice of the man who had repaired me. "What are you doing up? How did you get out of your room? Why didn't the guard stop you?"

I turn around to face the Foundation agents again. They are all still seated, but I can tell they are willing to stand up and catch me if necessary. A cursory scan of the room shows that there are no other exits or entrances here, which means that I cannot escape unless I find out how to break down this door behind me, which seems unlikely to happen.

Instead, I focus on the source of the voice, which my scanners indicate came from the man sitting on the far side of the table away from me. He is indeed the same man from before, because I recognize his scarred face and tall, thin body. He is wearing a simple, practical white coat, even though the room is warm enough to make a coat unnecessary.

As for the others, I recognize none of them except for Rozan —who looks similar to how he did before, only now without the robes. He instead is wearing a dwarfish leather jacket, while next to him sits Nacina, who looks exactly the same as I remember her. Scanners indicate that Rozan is still as angry as ever, as well as slightly confused, most likely by my presence. I do not see Palos, which makes me wonder where she is, although that is unimportant at the moment.

Seeing as I have nothing else to do and nowhere else to go, I simply say, "To answer your question, I escaped from the room you put me in by taking out the guards you set up to keep me in there. And, while I know you did not ask, the only reason I came in here is because one of those guards told me this would take me out of the building. It appears that that guard lied to me."

"Was it Garga?" says Rozan with a scowl. "I bet it was Garga."

"Yes, it was," I say. "Why do you ask?"

"Because that is exactly the sort of thing Garga would do," says Rozan. He gestures at the door behind me. "Dump his responsibility onto us, rather than do his freaking job. What an

56

idiot."

"I wouldn't say it turned out badly this time, however," says Nacina. She gestures at me. "After all, thanks to Garga's deception, we have now ensured that J997 will not escape."

I agree with Nacina. Looking back, it is obvious that Garga fooled me. I should have thought more deeply about how readily he 'helped' me. I should have interrogated him better, been more skeptical, but it does not matter anymore. I am stuck here, alone against a dozen of these Foundation agents, with the only possible escape route locked behind me.

My sensors do show, however, that there is a high concentration of skyras energy in this room. Most of the skyras energy appears to be radiating from a lone individual sitting at the table. I identify her as a witch, because she has the skyras rings that all Delanian witches do, although I do not know what magic she may be capable of.

"Are you going to apprehend me?" I ask the room at large, addressing no one in particular, because I do not know who is in charge. "Or are you going to destroy me? Either way, expect to face resistance from me."

I fully expect the Foundation agents to stand up and take me down. And my calculations state that they can defeat me easily, even though I know nothing about any of their abilities. Just the witch alone, who has more skyras energy than everyone else in this room, can defeat me without even trying. Still, my programming compels me to resist even in these situations, where logic dictates that I cannot win no matter how hard I fight.

Then the Foundation agents do something completely unexpected: They laugh.

Every one of them laughs. Rozan slams his fist against the table, laughing so hard he appears to have completely lost control over his laughter, while Nacina chuckles beside him. The powerful witch I noticed before is laughing a wild, wicked laugh that is at odds with her appearance, while the man who repaired me is laughing so hard he is slumped back in his chair, seemingly unable to stop even to breathe. The others also laugh as hard as their friends, which makes me wonder what I said that is so funny. After all, I did not tell a joke, so what do they find so humorous about what I just said?

I consult *Secrets of Humor*, which I have stored on the mobile Database, for answers, but I see nothing in the book about an audience spontaneously bursting into laughter after you make a very serious pronouncement. Maybe I had unintentionally told a Delanian joke? I know nothing about Delanian humor, after all, so it is possible I may have stumbled upon some obscure Delanian joke that I know nothing about.

Under ordinary circumstances, I would have used this as a distraction to make my escape, but unfortunately the door behind me is still locked by the skyras energy. All I can do, then, is wait until these people stop laughing. Hopefully then they will be able to explain what is so humorous about what I just said, although they are laughing so hard that it almost seems like they are going to laugh forever.

It takes them a few minutes, but soon all of the Foundation agents stop laughing. Even so, a handful of them still chuckle, as if they cannot get over the humor of my words.

"Expect to face resistance ... priceless," says Rozan, who chuckles every now and then. He nudges Nacina in the arm. "Isn't that the most hilarious thing you've ever heard, Naci? This machine clearly doesn't know a thing about us."

"Why did you all laugh?" I say, looking around at them all, hoping someone will explain. "I did not tell a joke. I merely stated a fact."

"We laughed because we know you couldn't beat us even if you tried," says Rozan. He gestures at his fellow agents, many of who are wearing smirks on their faces now. "You don't even know the power we command. Yeah, we know all about your ability to sense and calculate the amount of skyras in an area, but we've taken extra measures to make sure you can't know the true level of skyras energy in this place, which is far higher than you think."

I do not know if Rozan is telling the truth. Dwarves are well-known for their ability to tell convincing lies; in fact, once a fellow officer of mine was fooled by a dwarfish criminal on Xeeon who lied about his true identity. Rozan may well have been lying to me here in an attempt to destroy my morale.

On the other hand, his fellow agents are not disagreeing with him at all. Based on their facial expressions and body language, it appears that Rozan is telling the truth, although it is possible that they are all in on this lie in order to make it seem truer than it is.

I check my built-in lie detector, which all J bots are equipped with, but unfortunately I discover that it has been disabled. I do not recall having disabled it myself; in fact, until now, I did not know it is even possible to do so, because the built-in lie detector is an inherent feature in my class of robot.

The only logical explanation is that the mysterious man who repaired me earlier—the one sitting at the head of that table right

now, the one who ceased laughing more quickly than the others—
must have disabled it somehow. If so, then that means that this
man holds illegal knowledge of J bot engineering, which is
information only granted to certified technicians.

That the Foundation disabled my lie detector is a sign by itself
that they likely mean me harm. They do not want me to discover
the truth about them, whatever that is, and so have disabled the
best tool I have for discerning the truth.

I should attack these beings and attempt to make my escape. I
do not know for certain what their plans for me may be, but they
cannot be good, even if they do not intend on destroying me.

But then I stop and consider my situation. The witch by
herself can destroy me in one hit, if my scanners are reading her
skyras energy levels correctly (which I cannot be certain of, if
Rozan told the truth earlier), while the rest of these agents do not
look afraid of fighting me if necessary. That I am alone, with no
connection to the Database whatsoever aside from the mobile
version downloaded into my systems, gives me even less
incentive to attack them.

There is one thing I *can* do, however, and that is information
gathering. I might possibly be able to trick these agents into
telling me more about the Foundation, such as its aims and
origins, which in turn might be able to help me create a plan of
escape from here. It is not an ideal plan, but it is the only plan that
has even the remotest chances of succeeding at the moment, so I
must take what I can get.

That is, assuming they do not take me back to my room. There
is, after all, no reason for them to tell me anything. And as I have
no way to make them tell me anything, I may as well allow them

to take me away.

Therefore, I say, "Very well. I assume you will be apprehending me and sending me back to my room, as I am an escapee and that would be the most logical course of action for dealing with an escapee such as myself."

"Nah," says the mysterious man, shaking his head. He gestured at the room. "You are going to stay here, in this room."

I frown, which I understand to be a facial expression many organic beings often do to show their confusion, and say, "Why? I am not a member of the Foundation. Would it not be more logical to send me back to where I belong?"

"The Head has given us permission to tell you some things about us," said the man, "because, due to recent events, we are not allowed to let you leave this place. It would not be in your best interests, to say the least."

"Why?" I say. I step backwards before remembering that the door is still closed shut. "How do you know what my best interests are?"

"Because we figure that you probably don't want to be lynched by the angry mobs that believe you killed all those Knights of Se-Dela," says Rozan, leaning back in his chair, his dwarfish hands folded over his chest. "You know, those ones you worked with earlier?"

"I did not kill those Knights," I say. "It was Jornan ah Kona, the infamous criminal, who killed them. Why would you accuse me of that? Palos could tell you that I had no hand in murdering any of those Knights."

Mentioning Palos may not be the wisest thing I could have said, because as soon as her name leaves my mouth, Rozan glares at me and says, "What *Palos* says is irrelevant. It's what the *people* think about you that matters. And right now, public opinion isn't in your favor."

"Hold on," I say, holding up a hand. "I do not understand. Does the Delanian public believe that I murdered those Knights? Why?"

"We should start from the beginning," says the mysterious man, drawing the attention of everyone else in the room to him. "A lot has happened since Palos brought you here and we will tell you as much as you need to know, and no more."

I almost demand that they tell me everything, but then I look at it from their point of view. The Foundation is clearly some sort of secret organization, one that likely has many, many secrets that even all of these agents may not know of. It is only logical that they would withhold certain information from me, as I am not an ally or member of their group. And I should probably be thankful that they are giving me any information at all, rather than completely keeping me in the dark on it.

So I say, "All right. Tell me what you want to tell me. I have nothing else to do at the moment, after all, so I will listen while interrupting as little as possible."

"Good to know," says the man. "But first, let me introduce myself. My name is Konoa. And no, you won't be able to find that name in your mobile Database files, no matter how hard you look or whatever search terms you use, because I technically do not exist."

Konoa says that with a calm voice, although I can tell he is amused by his prediction of what I am about to do. Because the truth is, I am going to run his name through the mobile Database

ALLIANCE

and see if I have any information on him, but considering how all of the other Foundation agents I have met so far are not in the Database, this does not surprise me, either.

Still, I find his remarks cryptic, so I ask, "I do not understand. If you don't exist, how am I speaking with you right now?"

"It's a figure of speech, clicker," says Rozan, before Konoa can answer. He gestures at everyone sitting at the table. "*None* of us exist. Of course, you stupid robots don't understand things like metaphors and similes, right? I see why the Xeeonites think you're so advanced."

I do not debate Rozan's notion that metaphorical speech is usually a primary weakness in us J bots. In recent years, of course, we J bots have received upgrades to our language recognition software to allow us to understand figures of speech better, but we are still sometimes thrown off by them, especially if they happen to be newly-created slang.

But I can recognize sarcasm with no trouble, and I hear the sarcasm in Rozan's voice quite well. I also recognize the word 'clicker,' which is a derogatory word for robots, although I am not offended by it because I lack the ability to feel offended by anything.

"What it means, J997," says Konoa, who glares at Rozan briefly before returning his attention to me, "is that when you join the Foundation, all traces of your previous life are erased. Birth certificates are burned, family ties are cut, names are changed, Database entries are deleted ... from society's point of view, we are an organization of individuals who do not exist."

That explains why I am unable to find files on any of these Foundation agents in the mobile Database, but I find the last thing

63

he mentions alarming. "Did you say that Database entries are deleted? How so? Only authorized J bots and J bot technicians are allowed to alter or delete any Database entries, and even they have to fill out lengthy reports and papers explaining in detail why they have to before the Database gives them permission to do what they want."

"That's one of those things that we're not allowed to tell you," says Konoa. He folds his hands over the papers before him. "Now, why don't we change the subject to the Foundation itself?"

"Yes, I would like to know more about the Foundation," I say. I gesture at the room, which is actually my attempt to gesture at the whole building. "What are you aims? Your origins? How many members do you have? And who is your leader?"

"You asked pretty much all of the questions we're not *supposed* to answer," says Rozan, rolling his eyes. "You might as well ask us to give you our secret names, too."

"As Rozan said, we cannot answer any of those questions," says Konoa. "What we can tell you, however, is that the Foundation is an old organization with origins that stretch back eons. And we are ultimately a force for righteousness, so do not fear that we are up to evil."

"Conjecture," I say. "You have offered no proof to me that you Foundation agents have noble intentions. Based on the way you have treated me, I suspect you are up to no good."

"Yeah," says Rozan, leaning back in his chair and propping his boots on the table, his smile showing his dirty teeth. "Saving your hide from Jornan and then repairing you and recharging your energy … what horrible people we are. I see why you clickers are considered so intelligent; that's the kind of master logic that only

Waran-Una's personal pupils ever display. You have blown me away with your reasoning skills, good sir."

The sarcasm is evident in Rozan's voice. It does not irritate me, but I do find it a waste of time, as he does not tell me anything new about the Foundation.

"What Rozan means is that we have indeed treated you well," says Konoa. He gestures at my legs. "We repaired your leg, for example. If we had ill intentions for you, we would have scrapped you or thrown you out for the public to destroy. We know you are innocent of any crimes accused of you, which is why we have brought you here."

Konoa sounds quite sincere, far more sincere than sarcastic Rozan, but I am still suspicious. After all, as Konoa himself says, the Foundation does not exist in the Database, which instantly makes them suspicious to me. It is impossible to trust someone who I know nothing—and can know nothing—about.

But the fact is, this is exactly what I have been waiting for, so I say, "Okay. Please tell me more about the Foundation. Or what you are allowed to tell me, anyway."

"All right," says Konoa. He glances at the papers before him, like they are note cards he is reading from, before returning his gaze to look at me. "As I said, the Foundation is an ancient, but benevolent, organization. We have existed for eons and have worked behind the scenes for many years, with very few ever knowing of our existence outside of the organization itself."

"Are you affiliated with any governments?" I ask. "Do you work with King Waran-Una, for example? Are you allied with the Knights of Se-Dela or the Just Order of Witches and Wizards?"

"We are associated with no one but ourselves," says Konoa. "I mean, of course, we have agents in all of those organizations who keep us up-to-date on the various happenings within those groups, but officially we have no allies. It is the only way we can do what we do, as our secrecy allows us to do things that public organizations cannot."

Konoa speaks in a way that makes it seem like he expects me to agree with him. The other agents are nodding along, as if to confirm what he is saying, but I find the lack of accountability that this Foundation has to be problematic, to say the least. He may claim that his organization is benevolent, but he offers no proof or evidence to support that claim.

Still, logic dictates that this is not a good time to argue with these agents about the morality of their organization. First, I must gather information; then I can act.

"What type of threats does the Foundation typically battle?" I ask. "Criminals? Terrorists? Out of control wildlife? Natural disasters? What?"

"A little bit of all of that," says Konoa. "But our true conflict is with another organization that is as old as ours. It is that organization that Jornan ah Kona also belongs to, the same group that has framed you for the murder of all of those innocent Knights you were working with."

"What is this organization called?" I ask. "Can you tell me that?"

"It is one of the few things that the Head approves of us answering, so yes," says Konoa. "The name of this other organization is Reunification. And unlike us, they are actually up to no good; no, I would say they are even planning to do evil, which is why we fight against them."

ALLIANCE

As I always do, I run the name 'Reunification' through the mobile Database, even though by now I am starting to suspect that this is a pointless chore. And it is, because the term comes up with no results.

So I say, "What evil is this 'Reunification' planning to do?"

"That's information we can't give you at the moment," says Konoa. "But rest assured that, if they succeed, it will cause untold suffering for billions of people on both Dela and Xeeo. Trust me on that."

I do not see how I am supposed to trust someone who refuses to give me the full and complete facts about this, but I decide that I will do more investigating later. Who knows, maybe I will even get a chance to speak with an actual Reunification member, who may be able to tell me what their true goals are.

"Now I believe we have told you all we are allowed to tell you," says Konoa. "So I hope you have a better understanding of the situation you are in."

"Barely," I say. I gesture at myself. "You still have not explained what you mean when you say that I was 'framed' for the murder of those Knights. How could I be framed? When did this happen? How do I know you are telling the truth?"

"Ah, yes," says Konoa. He nods at the witch. "Will you please show J997 his wanted poster?"

The witch, without saying a word, taps a piece of paper on the table in front of her. As soon as she does, the paper vanishes into thin air, only to reappear a second later in front of me. I catch it before it falls to the ground and then peer at it more closely.

It is a thin sheet of paper, brown and wrinkly, as if it had been balled up at some point. In the center of it is an artist's sketch of me, and quite an accurate one, too. It even has the tiny dent above my left optic, the one I have never been able to get rid of. It is a sketch of my head, and nothing more, but the head is all I need to see that it is indeed supposed to be me.

Underneath my picture is my identification number—J997, in large, blocky letters—followed by a string of digits that is supposed to be my bounty, which is apparently 20,000 delanes according to this poster. I quickly convert the 20,000 delanes to Xeeonite digits and discover that it is roughly 30,000 Xeeonite digits; a fairly high number for any individual bounty.

I look up from the poster and notice how the Foundation agents are watching me, as if awaiting my response. I do not know what response they expect from me; maybe rage, but if so, they are going to be disappointed, because I cannot feel anger at all.

"Well, I see that this poster appears to be legitimate," I say, rolling it up into a tube as I speak. "But I still do not understand why everyone believes that I killed those Knights. I thought everyone would blame their deaths on Jornan and her lizard humanoid servants, not on me."

"Because by the time the bodies were found, Jornan and her minions were long gone," says Konoa. He sighs. "The other Knights who investigated the murders of their brethren noticed that you were missing and unaccounted for. Because the wounds on the corpses look like the kind of wounds a robot would inflict on a human, they assumed you did it."

"That still does not make sense to me," I say. "Are they ignoring Jornan now, even though she was also there when they were killed?"

"They aren't just blaming you," says Konoa. "The official story is that you and Jornan worked together to kill the Knights. Either you joined Jornan entirely out of your own free will or you were reprogrammed by her to help her and fled after killing the Knights you were working with; in either case, you are wanted by the Knights of Se-Dela and most of the Delanian public hates you."

"But what about my fellow J bots and the Xeeonite government?" I ask. "Do they know about my disappearance? Do they agree with the Knights' conclusion? Have they sent anyone to try to find me?"

"A few J bots were sent to aid in the investigation when it became clear you were missing," says Konoa. "They disagreed with the conclusion, but have been unable to offer an alternative explanation for your disappearance. So they returned to Xeeo, where the Database has decided that you are not worth the trouble of rescuing."

That I understand. In addition to being the largest electronic archive on Xeeo, the Database also acts as the Chief of the J bots, as our leader, making decisions for the whole force, not just a few J bots here and there. That the Database has apparently decided that I am no longer worth rescuing is grim news, but understandable, because if what the Foundation agents say is true, then I doubt very much that my fellow J bots can find me even if they try their hardest.

"But what about Sir Alart?" I say. "Surely he can vouch for my innocence, can't he? That is, if he survived against Jornan and her minions."

"Sir Alart did indeed survive and in fact is the Knight who

69

started the investigation, because he initially discovered the corpses of his allies," says Konoa. He flips through some of his papers, which appears to be a habit more than anything. "Sir Alart has argued for your innocence, but no on believes him, especially since he was not there to witness whether you did or did not kill them. He may be the only ally you have on this world, but that doesn't mean much."

I say nothing in response to that. It's good that Sir Alart is defending me, but I understand why Konoa does not think much of it.

"So if you were to walk out of this building and make your way back to, say, Ra-Dela, you would be arrested on the spot by any Knights on duty," says Konoa. "Or maybe get captured by a greedy bounty hunter looking for a quick delane on your way there. So I hope you understand why we cannot let you leave, at least right now."

"I understand," I say, nodding. "But that does not mean I think you made the right decision. I can prove my innocence because I recorded the details of that night in my head, in my memory banks."

I tap the side of my head as I say, "All I need to do is return to Xeeo and reconnect with the Database. It will then be able to display my memories of the incident onto a telescreen, which we can then show to the Knights of Se-Dela to clear my name. A brilliant plan, yes?"

Unfortunately, none of the Foundation agents appear entirely excited about my plan, even though it seems entirely rational and foolproof to me. That tells me that there must be some other variable I am overlooking, but what it is, I do not know.

ALLIANCE

Then Konoa looks down at his papers and says, "While that is certainly not the worst plan I have ever heard, it is unlikely to work."

"Unlikely?" says Rozan. He laughs. "I'd say it's *impossible* to work, given the circumstances."

"Impossible?" I repeat. "Why would you say that? After all, this is not merely hearsay. I can offer actual footage of the night when the lizard creatures attacked us. There is no way that any reasonable being could possibly dispute my story if they see my memories."

"I said 'given the circumstances,'" Rozan says. He rubs his forehead. "And given the current circumstances, the peoples of Dela are likely to think you doctored the footage to make yourself appear innocent, while the peoples of Xeeo will defend you. I'm not saying this could lead to a war between worlds, but—"

"It won't, although I doubt it will help relations between the worlds, either," says Konoa, glaring at Rozan as if to tell him to shut up. "The problem is that the Delanians are pretty skeptical of recorded footage of any sort. As Rozan said, they will think you altered it to make you appear innocent, and I doubt any of them will listen to any arguments to the contrary."

What Konoa says is true. I know for a fact that most Delanians do not trust Xeeonite recording tech, even though many Delanians are eager to use our other types of technology for their own uses. Konoa's warning is worth listening to, even though it paints his own people in a bad light (assuming Konoa is even Delanian; while he does appear to speak Delan very well, that does not mean he is a native of this world).

"Also," Rozan adds, "you've recorded some memories of

71

Palos, who, like the rest of us, technically doesn't even exist. Letting you go out and show everyone your memories would expose us, which isn't a real possibility for us at the moment."

"Is that the true reason you do not want to let me go?" I ask, folding my arms across my chest. "Because you do not want the rest of society to find out about you?"

"It is one reason," says Konoa, nodding. "The Head has worked hard to keep us under the radar and she does not want all of her hard work undone by a single robot like yourself."

"But if you are indeed good, then why operate in the shadows?" I ask. "Why not work directly with the J bots and the Knights of Se-Dela, among other public organizations dedicated to fighting for justice? They might be useful allies in your conflict with Reunification."

"You're starting to ask questions we can't answer again," says Rozan. "You know that, don't you?"

I frown. "I do now, although that does not erase the validity of my questions."

"It may very well not," says Konoa, "but as Rozan says, we can't answer that. You'll just have to trust us."

"I cannot fully trust people or organizations that do not exist in the Database," I say. I reach behind myself and feel the door, but it is still locked by the witch's skyras energy. "Not until you tell me everything about this organization, even though I know you won't."

"We don't need to," says Rozan. He rests his short legs on the floor and leans forward, resting his elbows on the table as he looks at me. "After all, you aren't even an agent like the rest of us. You're just a guest, and an annoying one at that."

"Then what will you do with me?" I ask. I gesture at the stone room we all stand in. "Put me in another room with magic straps? Keep me as your prisoner in this place? Will I ever be allowed to leave this building under my own free will?"

"Only the Head can answer that," says Konoa. "But for now, yes, you have to stay here. You know too much about us that it would be foolish for us to let you go, even if we wiped your memory clean first."

"But I must report back to the Database," I say. "I do not think you Foundation agents understand how urgent it is for me to do so."

"We don't care," says Rozan, rolling his eyes. "Now, we've answered your questions, so I think it's time we put you back where you—"

Rozan is interrupted by a powerful surge of skyras in this room that even I can tell is not from any of the Foundation members present here. Before I can locate the surge's source, a massive pinkish light bursts into existence over the table. Its sudden appearance causes some of the agents to jump out of their seats, although I notice that Konoa and the witch stay seated, despite the astonished expressions on their faces.

The pink light floats in the air for a brief period before morphing into the form of a vaguely human woman. She looks down on the agents seated around the table, while ignoring me. Scanners indicate that the giant pink woman is made of pure skyras energy, a phenomenon which I have never seen before in person, although I am aware that some Delanian magic users can conjure these kinds of 'skyras ghosts,' as they call them.

Then the skyras ghost says, in an unusually loud voice,

73

"Konoa, Rozan, everyone! There has been an attack on the Xeeonite branch. Xeeonite agents are flooding into the base by the dozens. Every agent currently within HQ must report to the Tower immediately!"

"What?" says Konoa in shock. "Ma'am, what is—"

"No time to explain," says the skyras ghost. She puts her hands together, like she is begging them to help. "You can speak to Lanresia, who is the only survivor in any shape to talk. But you must hurry, because she is dying even as we speak."

Chapter 5

As soon as the pink lady says that, she vanishes into nothingness, leaving behind nothing to indicate she even existed aside from a higher level of skyras energy lingering in the room, although my scanners say that even that is rapidly dissipating.

Before I can ask who that woman is or what she means, Konoa and the other agents stand up. I expect them to run toward the door, but instead, Konoa says to the witch, "Rina, teleport us to Tower. We have no time to lose."

The witch, whose name must be Rina, raises her left hand, but before she teleports them away, I step forward and say, "Wait. What is going on? What are you going to do with me? Are you just going to leave me here or may I come as well?"

Rozan tosses me an irritated glare. "You're not even an agent. Why do you think we'd take you with us? *You* weren't summoned, after all."

"Actually, I think he can come with us if he wants," says Konoa. He nods at me. "He's a good robot, so I doubt he'll cause us any harm. Besides, we don't have time to put him back in his room, so we might as well bring him with us, where we can keep an eye on him."

Konoa must have more authority over his fellow agents than I initially thought, because none of the other agents argue or disagree with him. Rozan rolls his eyes about this decision, but like the rest of them he does not disagree.

Without any further objections from the others, the witch known as Rina snaps her fingers. Then the room changes so abruptly that at first my sensors fail to indicate that our surroundings have changed at all, even though I can tell that they have.

We are standing inside a massive, wide-open chamber, with cobblestone walls, floor, and ceiling just like the last room we were in. Only this time, rather than having a large round table in the center of the room, there is an unusually large Crossways Portal standing on a slightly raised platform. It appears to be made out of stone, as most Delanian Portals tend to be, and is currently active, based on the fact that I can see the odd textures and strange green-and-purple portal within the ring itself.

But we are not alone in this room. People of various species—ranging from humans to the bird-like Checrom—are exiting the Portal and being guided toward the exit on the far end of the room by other people, who are probably Foundation agents, although their lack of any uniform or identifying symbols makes that hard for me to confirm. Still, the fact that all of them are here is proof enough of their allegiance.

The people coming from the Portal appear wounded and afraid. One of them, a male human, limps along, while a female

Checrom has most of her feathers burned off and her beak chipped at the tip. Another person, this one a female human, steps through the portal and immediately falls face forward, but is caught in time by Rina, who I did not realize had teleported over there to catch her just in time.

One of the injured Foundation agents—because that is who these people must be, if the Head's message is accurate—carried past me is a male Jikorian with three deep gashes in his chest. He is completely unconscious, but I do a quick scan of him anyway as his handlers pass me.

Scanners indicate that the Jikorian male is a Xeeonite, because I detect several implants in his body, among them a camera in his left eye that he likely uses to take pictures with. But I do not learn much else about him, because soon he is taken out of the room through the large double doors at the other end, although where he is taken, I do not know.

As I stand there, the other Foundation agents who teleported with me move to help their injured comrades. Even Konoa goes to help, but before he does, a feminine voice says, "Konoa!"

Both Konoa and I look in the direction of that voice. A human woman is walking toward us, passing the long line of Foundation agents who are transporting their injured allies out of the room. Even so, she looks at each wounded agent as they pass, even mutters what sounds like a prayer under her breath, but I cannot tell what she mutters because it is in a language I do not recognize.

My first impression is that this woman is human, but as she walks closer to us, the information my scanners give me make no sense. She has an unusually high skyras energy level, much higher than even Rina's, but she has no rings on her fingers with which to hold her skyras. What makes her skyras level so remarkable is that she should be unable to so much as walk with all of that energy flowing through her, but she moves as easily as anyone else in the room. If anything, she appears to move even more gracefully than the others.

Another thing I notice about her is her body. Her back appears much larger and swollen than the rest of her body, although with her silver robes I am unable to determine if that is a natural part of her anatomy or if it is somehow a mechanical implant or magical distortion. Even my scanners can't identify it.

And like with all of the Foundation agents (of which there appear to be many, based on the amount of agents flooding in from the Portal and the amount of agents aiding those agents in leaving this room), I find no files on her in the mobile Database at all. At this point, I am tempted to stop using the mobile Database entirely, although that is nothing but an idle thought.

"Ma'am," says Konoa, turning to face the woman as she approaches. He bows deeply, which tells me that this woman must be highly important. "What happened? Why are so many of our Xeeonite brethren so badly injured?"

"Lanresia will tell us," says the woman as she approaches us. "I'll take you to her."

I raise a hand. "May I come with you two? I would also like to learn what happened, even though I am not a Foundation agent."

The woman stops and looks at me carefully with her blue eyes, like I am a possible threat. Her fingers twitch, like she is going to cast a spell on me, but she does nothing.

Instead, she nods and says, "If you wish."

Then she turns and walks toward the exit again. Konoa and I follow, although I notice Konoa keeps looking back at the Portal and seemingly-endless stream of injured Foundation agents coming from it (although I notice that the stream is thinning). He must care very deeply about his fellow agents, which adds more evidence to my theory that Konoa is a high-ranking member of this organization.

It does not take us long to leave the room and enter a hallway similar to the one I had been in earlier, only slightly wider and with more people. The Delanian agents are taking their Xeeonite counterparts into what appears to be a medical room on the other side of the hall, but the woman does not lead us into that room.

Instead, she turns to the right and walks a few feet before stopping in front of a plain-looking stone door. She pushes the door open and enters without hesitation, followed by Konoa, and then myself.

The room we enter is almost too small after the wide-openness of the Portal room. It reminds me of the room they kept me in when I was first taken here, only it is a little bigger and personable, with a bookshelf along one wall and a bed with white sheets up against the opposite wall.

On the bed lies an elf, but she is not a Delanian elf. While she is tall and has clear skin, like most elves, she is also bald, a trend among Xeeonian woman that pegs her as a Xeeonite native. Another hint is her speaking snake, a machine attached to her waist like a belt that is designed to speak for her, which means she must be a mute.

The elf herself is injured, although not as badly as some of the other Foundation agents I saw earlier. A cut runs along the bridge of her nose, while her left arm is broken and in a sling now. One of the speaking snake's optics has been burned out, although aside from that burned out optic, the rest of the machine appears perfectly functional.

The elf looks up at us when we enter. She smiles at Konoa, but then looks at me in confusion.

"Who is that?" says the elf, although it is actually her speaking snake that speaks, its voice more mechanical and monotone than an organic's voice. "I have never seen him before."

"He's a ... guest," says the woman, who glances at me when she says that. "Don't worry. You can trust him as much as you can trust me."

Lanresia relaxes, which tells me that she must trust this woman a great deal.

As for Konoa, he is at Lanresia's side before I even realize it. He grabs her hand and holds it tightly, his eyes focused exclusively on Lanresia, like he thinks he might never see her again. Scanners indicate that his pheromone levels are quite high, although that is irrelevant to our current situation, so I do not focus on it.

"Lanresia, my love," says Konoa, never taking his eyes off her for even a second. "I was so worried when I heard you were injured, but I am glad to see you have survived."

"I'm happy to see you, too, Konoa," says Lanresia, her pheromone levels as high as his. "I thought for sure I was going to be a goner there, but thankfully I managed to escape before they could kill me."

I look at the woman, who now has her arms folded across her

chest, and ask, "Why did you put Lanresia in this room separate from the other agents?"

"Because I want to be the first to know about what happened on Xeeo," says the woman, without looking at me. "Then I will tell the others, who are already frightened and stressed by this sudden and unexpected turn of events. The truth, whatever it is, will worsen their stress, so it is better I hear the story first so I can deliver it later, after this situation becomes less stressful."

I cock my head to the side. "Are you the Head?"

The woman nods, still keeping her eyes on Lanresia and Konoa. "Yes. But that does not matter at the moment. What matters is Lanresia's story. Lanresia, will you tell us what happened?"

Lanresia looks at the Head and me, although even I can tell she would rather continue to stare into Konoa's eyes than talk about her experiences. Scanners indicate that Lanresia's stress levels—which had dropped noticeably when Konoa entered the room—are rising again, rising much higher than is healthy for your average elf according to Database records on typical stress levels for elves.

"It was ... horrible," says Lanresia with a shudder. "I don't want to talk about it at all, but I will anyway, because I don't want a repeat here of what happened there."

"Her stress levels are rising quite high," I say. "While I am no med-bot, I question the wisdom of having her relate her experiences so soon after the traumatic event she just experienced."

"I'll be fine," says Lanresia, waving at me with her other hand. "I just need a moment to figure out where to start."

"That's fine, my love," says Konoa, who strokes her other hand gently. "Take your time. We don't want to stress you out too much."

Lanresia goes silent and appears to be thinking. Then she says, "Well, I should get straight to the point: The Xeeonite HQ was attacked by a group of humanoid lizard creatures that can breathe fire."

"Humanoid lizard creatures?" I repeat, unable to stop myself. "Did they, by chance, resemble—"

"J997," says the Head, glaring at me. "Don't interrupt her. Save your questions for when she finishes her story."

I have no reason to listen to the Head, as she has no authority over me, but I decide to do so because it is better to listen and get the facts first, rather than ask questions that may not need to be asked. Besides, there is something about the way the Head looks at me that tells me I will become scrap metal if I continue to interrupt Lanresia's story with my questions.

Lanresia takes a deep breath and continues her story. "We don't know how the lizard creatures got in. We know they started in the lower levels, where the Energy Center is. They destroyed our generator, which caused the power to go out. Then they made their way up to the higher levels, killing anyone they ran into."

"How many agents did they kill?" asks the Head, taking a step closer to Lanresia, rubbing her hands together anxiously. "Was Kojama killed?"

"I don't know the exact number," Lanresia admits. She wipes sweat from her forehead. "And I don't know about Kojama, either. We tried to fight the monsters, but they were too strong and we didn't know what to expect. I managed to save a lot of agents, but there was so much confusion that I am not certain how many died and how many lived."

I want to ask who this 'Kojama' is, but none of the Foundation agents around me seem likely to answer my questions. Better to listen and learn what happened and ask later, if I get a chance.

"What about the human Knight?" the Head asks. I notice a tone of concern in her voice. "Rii? The one you elves call Apakerec?"

"Last I saw, he was in one of the medical rooms resting," says Lanresia. "But I think he died, because that particular hallway he was in was where the worst slaughter happened and none of the other agents reported seeing him or finding his body. I'm sorry."

I search the mobile Database records for information on this 'Rii Apakerec,' and much to my relief, I find a file about this Rii. The mobile Database claims that he is a Knight of Se-Dela, but unfortunately, the mobile Database does not tell me much else about him. He must not be an important Knight, then, although how he ended up in the Xeeonite branch of the Foundation, I do not know.

"It is fine, Lanresia," says Konoa, still stroking her hand. "We know you did your best. Thanks to your bravery, you saved the lives of … excuse me, Head, but do you know how many Xeeonite agents have arrived so far?"

"Thirty," says the Head, "though more are still coming."

"Thirty lives, Lanresia," says Konoa, looking at her with warm eyes. "If we could have saved Rii as well … but no matter. You've done as much as you can. Now it is time for you to rest."

"Not until she answers the rest of our questions," says the Head, shaking her head. "Now, Lanresia, did you discover anything else? Do you know who sent those creatures?"

"I don't know for sure," Lanresia admits. The voice of her speaking snake glitches slightly, although it is barely perceptible and I doubt anyone other than myself caught it. "But I strongly suspect it was Reunification. They're the only ones who could possibly have tracked down our HQ and sent those evil beasts; the only ones, in fact, who would even try to do such a thing, seeing as no one else even knows about us."

"But how could Reunification have discovered the location of our Xeeonite HQ?" asks Konoa. He looks at the Head, like he expects her to have the answer.

The Head shakes her head. "I don't know. Maybe there is a spy among us who leaked our location to the enemy, or maybe the Founder used some of his foul magic to find us or maybe they captured one of our agents and got that information from him. In any case, this is a terrible turn of events that even I did not foresee, because Reunification is rarely this direct."

"They must be getting confident," says Konoa. "But why? Unless they are—"

"Konoa, we will discuss this matter later," says the Head, interrupting him before he can finish speaking. "For now, we need to let Lanresia rest. She has told us as much as we need to know. Our next course of action is to prepare for the next assault, which will no doubt be on this base."

"You think so, ma'am?" asks Konoa as he lets go of Lanresia's hand.

"It is only logical," says the Head. "I know the Founder. He is never one to do anything by half-measures. If he destroyed the Xeeonite branch, he will assuredly attempt to destroy this one as well, although when or how, I do not know."

Konoa's face pales and he glances at Lanresia. I understand his fear, even though I am unable to feel that emotion. Considering how badly the Xeeonite agents are injured from that assault, there is no doubt that a similar massacre can occur here if the Foundation agents are not prepared for it.

Despite that, I still have questions to ask. Lanresia appears to have finished her story now, so I decide this is as good a time as any to ask the questions on my mind.

"Lanresia described humanoid lizard creatures attacking the Xeeonite agents," I say. I look at the elf, who now looks as though she can barely remain awake. "Lanresia, did these creatures look like humanoid Great Lizards?"

"Yes," says Lanresia, her speaking snake nodding along with her. "Why?"

"I see," I say, stroking my chin. "Then it appears that the lizard creatures that attacked me earlier and killed those Knights I was working with likely belong to the same species as those that attacked you Xeeonites."

Lanresia looks up at Konoa in surprise. "Konoa, what does this J bot mean? What's happened since I was last here? And, for that matter, why is there a J bot in our base at all? Is he a new agent?"

"No, my love, J997 is not a new agent," says Konoa. He glances at me, like he is not sure he can trust me. "He's ... well, he's a guest, I suppose you could say, who was targeted by Reunification. We're keeping him here for safety reasons."

I hardly call myself a 'guest' of these people, seeing as I was taken here against my will and am not allowed to leave. If anything, I believe I am a prisoner, although one that they allow to walk around with more freedom than your typical prisoner, I suppose.

Before I can correct Konoa's inaccurate description of me, the Head says, "In any case, J997 is most likely correct about the monsters that attacked him and the monsters that attacked our base belonging to the same species. After all, the monsters that had attacked J997 were working for Jornan, who is also an agent of Reunification. That still does not answer *what* those creatures are, however."

"Does it matter?" asks Konoa, who grabs at his hair nervously. "I heard Palos's description of the beasts. And if they managed to take the Xeeonite HQ from us, then there's a good chance they'll get us here, too."

"Unless we prepare for it," says the Head, who in contrast to Konoa is quite cold. "We still have many good agents on hand here. As long as we do not panic, we should be fine."

"But why did they choose to attack *now*?" asks Konoa. "Are they that close to completing the Mission already?"

"I don't know," says the Head, shaking her head. "All I know is that we must prepare for the worst in case they learn of the location of this base."

As soon as those words leave her mouth, there are several hard knocks at the door that make us jump in surprise. Then the door bursts open and Rozan enters, almost falling over his feet, but he hangs onto the doorknob to balance himself.

"Madam Head!" says Rozan, breathing hard like he just ran a mile. "Monsters coming through the Portal and attacking everyone!"

"Monsters?" Konoa repeats. "What monsters?"

Wiping the sweat off his bald head, Rozan says, "Large, humanoid lizards. Sharp claws, and some of them can breathe fire, too, the bastards."

"Then shut the Portal off," the Head snaps.

"We can't, madam," Rozan says, shaking his head so hard it looks like it might pop off. "We think the monsters are using the Xeeonite Portal to force ours open, meaning we cannot turn it off from this side."

"By the Old Gods," says the Head, rubbing her forehead in exasperation. Then she gestures at Konoa. "Go and help the others. We need every able-bodied agent out there to beat back the invaders before they get too deep into the base."

"Yes, ma'am," says Konoa, who bows at the Head and darts out the door, almost knocking Rozan over, before anyone else can say anything.

"What about me?" I say, pointing at myself. "May I go help? I know I am not an agent of the Foundation, but I am in no mood to allow those creatures to overrun and destroy this place, and me with it."

The Head looks at me with skepticism in her eyes, like she does not believe me for even a second. I forgot how little the agents around here trust me, although I suppose the feeling is mutual, seeing as I only suggested to help because I do not want to be destroyed along with everyone else. I have no real care or concern for the agents personally; as a matter of fact, I suspect they may be criminals, if their secretive behavior is any indication.

Then she sighs heavily and, pointing toward the open door,

says, "Fine. Go and aid my men however you see fit. But don't you dare use this opportunity to make an attempt to escape through the Portal back to Xeeo, if that's what you are thinking."

"In truth, that idea did not occur to me until you mentioned it," I say. "But you don't need to worry, because if Lanresia's report is true, then there is nothing awaiting me on the other side of that Portal except more of those violent, dangerous monsters that have already tried to destroy me once today."

Chapter 6

The scene in the Portal room has changed significantly since the last ten minutes, which according to my internal clock is how long it has been since I was last in there.

I notice that the floor is already littered with dead agents, some Delanian, some Xeeonite, although I cannot identify which branch of the Foundation they may have belonged to due to my unfamiliarity with both branches. Nonetheless, the sight of so many dead agents is not a good one by any definition of the word.

More of those strange lizard humanoids are emerging from the Portal, growling and snapping their teeth, slashing their claws through the air. Some agents—Delanians, most likely, as the Xeeonites were in no condition to fight against these invaders—are keeping the lizard humanoids away from the doors, having formed a thin line against the ever-increasing number of lizard humanoids that emerge from the Portal and fighting back as hard as they can.

Some of the still-living agents are using swords and axes to beat back any lizard humanoids within reach, while others—

wizards and witches—use magic to douse the creatures in fire or shock them with electricity or harm them in other ways. Despite that, however, it is quite clear that the agents are barely holding their own against these creatures and will likely be overwhelmed soon without backup.

Despite these grim odds, Konoa charges forward anyway (although that may be because he does not know how likely it is that he and his fellow agents will be overwhelmed soon). He does not even appear to have any weapons, which makes me wonder how he intends to battle these creatures without getting slaughtered like a lamb.

My question is answered when Konoa reaches the back of the line and one of the other agents hands him a short, blunt sword. Konoa then steps up next to his fellow agent and the two begin slicing viciously at any lizard humanoids that get within their reach, although it is still plainly only a matter of time before the lizard humanoids break through and overrun the whole base.

I should, perhaps, go and join them at the line. Scanners indicate my power source is still at 87%, which means I can fight for hours without worrying about breaking down, but that will be pointless because the lizard humanoids keep coming through the Portal.

Therefore, if we are to deal with this issue once and for all, I must find a way to disable the Portal that the lizard humanoids are coming from. If I can shut it off, I can cut off the number of lizard humanoids to a manageable size, which will make them that much easier to deal with.

And disabling the Portal may not even be a difficult job; while Rozan's report about the lizard humanoids on the other side forcing it open may be correct, the mobile Database has detailed records on how Delanian Portals work. By reading those records, I should be able to find a way to disable the Portal permanently from our side; assuming, of course, I can make it that far.

Aside from the line of Foundation agents in my path, there are also the lizard humanoids themselves, who no doubt will try to stop me from shutting down that Portal.

Nonetheless, I must try, because I am the only one in any position to do it. The doors behind us are closed and it does not seem like any other agents will get here in time to help, although even if they do, their help will not be very useful if the Portal is still active.

Thus, I jump into the air and activate the jet boosters on my feet. The boosters send me flying through the air over the line of agents defending the base from the ever-growing army of lizard humanoids, while the lizard humanoids themselves look up at me in surprise, like they did not expect me to do this.

I don't pay them any attention, however, because my optics are focused entirely on the Portal in the center of the room. As long as I can reach it, I—

Flames shoot up through the air, enveloping me before I even realize what is happening. Scanners indicate that my exterior temperature is rising rapidly, too rapidly for my body to handle.

I swerve to the right and emerge from the flames, but my body temperature is still too hot (though it is cooling quicker the longer I stay out of the flames). I look at the fire and see that at least six of the lizard humanoids are breathing the flames that nearly overheated my systems, probably in an attempt to melt me into slag.

Then I hear the roar of one of the lizard humanoids and look in the direction I am flying. One of the humanoids is jumping at me, somehow having made the jump despite the fact that I am several feet off the ground.

And it is too late for me to swerve out of the way, although I try to do so at the last minute. The creature slams into me in midair and we both fall to the floor on top of all of the lizard humanoids underneath us.

The fall is abrupt, and before I can recover, the other lizard humanoids are around me, grabbing and biting at me with their sharp claws and teeth. It does not hurt me at all, but I doubt it will be long before they tear me apart like tin.

So I activate the electrical barrier inside me. As soon as the barrier shoots out from my body, many of the lizard humanoids cry out in pain and retreat or, in a few cases, fall unconscious onto the floor, causing some of their fellow lizard humanoids to trip over them. Those who aren't close enough to be harmed by my barrier still retreat to a safer distance, watching me with intelligent reptilian eyes as if looking for an opening in which to strike.

But I do not give them the opening they are looking for. Instead, I hop to my feet and, still keeping the barrier active, run toward the Portal, forcing the other lizard humanoids around me to scatter to avoid being electrocuted. That means that these lizard humanoids are much smarter than I originally thought, which makes me wonder briefly again what they are.

A fiery *wooshing* sound is followed by flames appearing in my path, a continuous stream of fire breathed by one of the lizard humanoids. I skid to a stop because my sensors indicate that the fire is too hot for me to go through without sustaining severe damage to my exterior and interior.

I raise my hand to unleash my finger lightning bolts at the lizard humanoids, but before I can do so, more flames erupt behind me. A second later, even more flames appear to my left and to my right, effectively trapping me inside a box of fire.

Sensors indicate that all of these flames are too hot for me to try to run through. And because of the fire in my optics, I cannot easily locate the creators of the fire, especially with the flames drawing in ever closer and closer to me, giving me less room in which to maneuver.

But this is not an impossible situation. I activate my boosters and soar into the air once again, safely escaping the flames, although as soon as I do so, more of those lizard humanoids leap through the air toward me, howling with rage.

This time, however, I twist out of their way, allowing the lizard humanoids to fly past me. I then head for the Portal, from which lizard humanoids are still pouring, although there seem to be less and less because I see fewer and fewer of these lizard humanoids coming through the Portal.

Then I hear a cry of pain and look over my shoulder. Back toward the line of Foundation agents holding back the monsters, one of the agents is stabbed in the chest by one of the lizard humanoids, causing him to fall down, which creates an opening in the line that the other agents try to fill, although they are already so thinly spread out that they fail to do so. The lizard humanoids break through, separating the two sides as the lizard creatures make for the doors to the rest of the base while the surviving agents fight harder than ever to keep the lizard humanoids back.

But I still focus on the Portal. I cannot allow myself to be distracted by anything less important, even if it is more urgent.

Soon I land on the platform on which the Portal is built. A lizard humanoid pokes its head through the Portal before I punch it in the face, sending the monster tumbling back to where it comes from. I hear the lizard humanoids behind me coming to stop me, which means I do not have much time to figure out how to shut off this Portal.

According to the mobile Database records, Delanian Portals are powered by a built-in, continuously active power crystal that absorbs skyras energy from the environment around it. That means I need to locate the power crystal to shut it off, but at the moment I do not have the time to do so.

Instead, I rush at the Portal and slam my shoulder into its ring. The Portal shudders under the impact, but still remains standing and active, although I intend to correct that by pushing against the Portal as hard as I can.

Straining against the Portal, I check my power level to ensure that I am still at optimal levels. I am at 79%, which is still good, although unless I put all of my energy into pushing against this Portal, I may not be able to knock it down from its foundations.

Hence, I divert all remaining energy into my arms, legs, and shoulders, which causes my electrical barrier to shut off, but that is fine because I do not need it at the moment. As long as I am strong enough to shove this Portal down, I will be all right.

Then I hear the lizard humanoids behind me and I look over my shoulder. The lizard humanoids are climbing the steps toward me, their claws drawn and their teeth bared. But I do not have any energy left to deal with them because the rest of my energy is diverted into putting all of my strength into pushing this Portal over.

Rather than tear at me with their claws, however, the lizard humanoids stop as they surround me. Scanners indicate that their body temperatures are rising rapidly, which means they are going to unleash their fiery breaths on me again. And considering how high their temperatures are rising, I know I will be melted into slag if I do not move before they breathe their fire on me.

But I must continue to put all of my strength into knocking down this Portal. If I succeed in that objective, then the fall might shatter its power crystal, which will force it to shut off even if its Xeeonite counterpart on the other side is still active.

Yet if I continue to push and shove, the lizard humanoids will melt me into slag, which means I must move now if I want to avoid that fate.

Thus, I divert all of my energy into the boosters on the bottom of my feet and immediately go flying into the air. As I soar upwards, the lizard humanoids unleash their collective fire breaths on the spot of the Portal that I had been pushing against.

As I hover in the air, I watch as the flames—which are so hot I barely believe the temperature readings my scanners show me—cover the part of the Portal I had been shoving against. The flames are loud and noisy, but at least they are nowhere near me.

The lizard humanoids must realize I am no longer there, because they soon cut off their fire breaths and look up at me. They appear to be trying to figure out how to get me, but that does not matter to me because I now see the full damage that their fire breaths have caused to the Portal.

Their fire was so hot that it had burned straight through the

Portal's ring. The Portal itself blinks in and out of existence several times, but I now see an excellent opportunity to destroy not only the Portal, but these lizard humanoids as well.

I soar around the Portal and reach its backside, while the lizard humanoids that have attempted to turn me into slag follow my progress with their strangely intelligent eyes. Using both hands, I grab the top of the Portal's ring and shove it forward as hard as I can, using my boosters to give me extra momentum.

It works. The Portal—weakened by the flames from the lizard humanoids—teeters and totters before falling forward. As it falls, the Portal within immediately shuts off, turning it into a powerless and unusually large stone ring.

The lizard humanoids attempt to flee, and a few of them succeed, but most of them are crushed by the falling Portal, which lands on them with a *boom*. Not only that, but the impact causes the Portal to shatter into pieces, which creates a much louder crashing sound than I expected.

But I am satisfied with this, because the Portal has been shut off entirely now. Its Xeeonite counterpart is probably still active, but without this one to connect it, it is essentially useless without proper repairs.

The fall of the Portal is loud enough to cause many of the lizard humanoids and Foundation agents to stop the fighting and look at my handiwork. The lizard humanoids appear stunned by what I did, while the Foundation agents recover quickly from their initial surprise and begin hacking away at the closest lizard humanoids, killing a few before the lizard humanoids snap out of their shock and resume their fight with the agents.

Hovering in the air, I check my power levels briefly again. My systems indicate that I am at 77% now, despite all of the power I have used. That is more than enough power for me to aid the Foundation agents in killing off the rest of these lizard humanoids.

I soar down to the floor and land gracefully. As soon as my feet touch the floor, four of the lizard humanoids surround me. Scanners indicate they are angrier than ever now, with their body temperatures rising with their anger levels.

Nonetheless, I fire a finger lightning bolt at the one in front of me, striking it in the chest and forcing it to stagger back. Its brothers jump on me, but as soon as they do, I activate my electrical barrier, shocking them in midair and causing them to fall to the floor stunned.

Then I look around and notice how much more viciously the Foundation agents are fighting against the lizard humanoids. Konoa, for example, beheads one of the creatures and then kicks another in the face, while the agent fighting next to him tackles another humanoid to the floor and stabs it repeatedly in the throat. The destruction of the Portal must have boosted their morale, but I do not have time to stand here and think about this, because there are still many of these lizard humanoids trying to kill us and I must do what I can to help stop them.

Just as I take another step forward to aid the nearest agents, the doors to the room burst open, slamming into the lizard humanoids that are trying to break through it. Not even one second later, more Foundation agents pour through the doors, at least three dozen in all, carrying weapons of all sorts, and those that do not have any weapons have skyras rings glowing on their fingers.

The unexpected appearance of so many agents at once does not, however, surprise the lizard humanoids at all. Instead, they turn their attention from the few agents already in here and move to meet the reinforcements, although I can tell even now that they are unlikely to succeed.

As I watch, the reinforcements stab and slash at the lizard humanoids, dividing the creatures from each other and using magic to finish them off. Nacina, for example, beheads one of the lizard humanoids with her dead gray sword, while the witch Rina snaps her fingers and freezes another lizard humanoid inside a huge block of ice before Rozan smashes it with a hammer he carries.

While I still want to help, it becomes plain to me that any help I can render is unnecessary. This battle started with the agents outnumbered, but with the Portal now closed—and with it, any hope of the lizard humanoids of receiving back-up destroyed—the Foundation agents appear more than capable of finishing off the remaining lizard humanoids by themselves.

Therefore, I decide to take this opportunity to study the stunned ones around me, which are so still that they look dead, although my sensors indicate that they are still breathing. Ignoring the terrified and angry cries of the humanoid lizards and the swearing and magical blasts from the agents, I bend over the nearest stunned lizard humanoid and examine its body.

Studying your enemy in the middle of battle like this may seem foolhardy, but I wish to collect as much information on these creatures as possible so I can share it with my fellow J bots when I return to Xeeo. Besides, the Foundation is keeping the still-living lizard humanoids distracted, so I doubt any of them will attempt to attack me while I study this stunned one.

As carefully as possible, I scrap off a part of this lizard humanoid's skin and run it through my systems. Ordinarily, my scanners are used in the occasional detective work, such as when I am examining evidence at a crime scene, but they can scan just about anything and tell me what it is, regardless of whether it has anything to do with a crime scene I am investigating or not.

Scan complete. According to the skin sample I scanned, these creatures do indeed have Grand Lizard and human DNA in them. While these creatures are most definitely unique in that regard, this confirms my theory that these creatures are the result of gene-splicing, a science still in its infancy in Xeeo, but which is rapidly becoming popular due to its possible uses in the medical field.

That does not explain, however, how Reunification created these creatures. From what I have read about gene-splicing, it is still far too new of a science for anything even remotely this complicated to be created. That Reunification has made so many of these lizard humanoids means that they must possess scientific knowledge and understanding that even Xeeo's brightest do not. If so, that makes Reunification even more dangerous than I thou—

The eyes of the lizard humanoid, the one I have been studying, open without warning. My own optics register that in less than a second, but before I can react, the lizard humanoid stabs me directly in the chest with one of its claws.

This time, the lizard humanoid's claw pierces my chest and tears through some of my inner-circuitry. My systems immediately begin working to find out what the damage is, but I have no time to waste waiting for what it finds, because the lizard humanoid is still tearing at my interior.

I shoot my twin eye beams at the lizard humanoid's face. The beams strike it in the face, burrowing through its forehead and into its brain. The lizard humanoid does not even cry out in pain before its head falls limply to the side and its body becomes still.

I grab its claw that is still embedded in my chest and gently remove it. The claw did not stab very far into my chest, but it is enough that I cannot simply ignore it. Perhaps I can have Konoa repair it, because despite his lack of certification, he seems unusually knowledgeable about repairing J bots.

System scan complete. Report indicates that nothing vital was destroyed or irreparably damaged by the lizard humanoid's claw, but I still need to have a certified J bot technician repair what was damaged as quickly as possible. My legs are still in working condition, so I stand up, but as soon as I do so, I hear something coming behind me.

Turning around, I see that it is another lizard humanoid, this one with blood covering its face (unable to ascertain whether that is its blood or the blood of one of the Foundation agents), as it charges me even faster than its brethren. I aim my fingers to shoot lightning bolts at it, but the lizard humanoid is faster than I can shoot.

It slams headfirst into my abdomen, causing me to stagger backwards. I trip over the lizard humanoid I killed and fall on my behind, but I take advantage of the fall and roll backwards out of the range of the lizard humanoid that had slammed into me.

Rising back to my feet, I aim my fingers at the creature again, but then it breathes a stream of fire at me. I jump aside to avoid being melted by the flames and then shoot my finger lightning bolts at the lizard humanoid.

The bolts strike the lizard humanoid dead on, causing it to collapse immediately. And a quick scan of its corpse tells me that it is indeed dead.

I glance around the area, but I do not see any other immediate threats nearby. Almost all of the lizard humanoids are dead now, having been slaughtered by the Foundation agents, while the surviving handful have been captured with thick steel chains around their wrists and ankles, their mouths shut tight with metal muzzles (though I am not sure where they got those muzzles).

As for the Foundation agents themselves, they do not seem to have suffered as many casualties as the lizard humanoids have. Some of the agents are dead—for example, a dwarf whose face is now little more than burnt meat—but the rest are alive, albeit wounded or injured in many ways. Still, it seems like the wounded will survive, especially now that the enemy is defeated.

The surviving lizard humanoids are dragged out of the room by some of the Foundation agents, while the rest stay behind to clean up the corpses of the ones they killed. They are far more efficient and quick than I expected them to be, because the agents waste no time in gathering the corpses into one large pile near the right side of the room, away from the corpses of their fallen fellow Foundation agents.

As they clean up the corpses, Konoa walks up to me. He still wields that short sword from before, although it is now covered in blood and his sweaty face is covered in scratches. His shirt has been ripped down the front, partially revealing his chest, but he looks better than I expected him to look after fighting so many of those vicious beasts.

"Thanks for destroying the Portal, J997," says Konoa. He

nods at the broken Portal, although it is a tired nod. "If you had not destroyed the Portal like that, we probably would have been completely overrun by those monsters."

I nod. "It is nothing. I only did what I had to do."

Then I gesture at the surviving monsters that are being hauled out of the room. "What will happen to the survivors?"

"That is information I am not at liberty to disclose to you," says Konoa. He shrugs sheepishly. "I mean, I would like to, since I think you deserve to know it after all of the help you've given us, but you are still technically not an agent, so I can't tell you that."

I nod, partly because I understand the need to keep certain things secret from outsiders, and partly because I suspect that the creatures are going to be dissected and examined by the Foundation's resident scientists. Or, since this is Dela, by their resident wizards and witches, although I do not know if they have any wizards or witches who specialize in dissecting living creatures.

So, changing the subject, I point at one of the dead agents, the dwarf from before, and ask, "And the dead agents? What will be done with them?"

"All of them will be given proper funerals, naturally enough," says Konoa. His shoulders slump and he sighs. "But that will have to be for later. Right now, the Head needs to know about our victory over the intruders, if she doesn't already. I also need to find out what her next orders for us are."

"By 'us,' are you including me as well?" I ask. I point at the floor. "Or am I supposed to return to my room several floors below?"

Konoa strokes his chin in thought. "Well, that depends mostly on what the Head wants, but I think it is likely that you will be returned to your room, yes."

"Even after I helped save your base from being overrun by these monsters?" I ask.

"Well, as I said, it really depends on what the Head wants," Konoa says. "Normal protocol is that visitors—when we *have* visitors, which we rarely do—usually aren't even *allowed* to wander around the base, much less help us fend off an unexpected enemy invasion. So I do not know for sure what the Head will have you do."

"But you think it is more likely that she will return me to my room," I say. "At least until this situation with Reunification is taken care of, yes?"

Konoa nods. "That is probably what she will tell us to do with you, yes."

I nod. "I understand. But first, I must tell you something, Konoa."

Konoa frowns and folds his arms across his chest. "And what is that?"

I lash out, punching Konoa in the face. The blow knocks Konoa off his feet, but I catch him before he can fall to the floor and then turn him around to face the other agents, who now notice me holding their fellow agent against his will.

Just as I expected, the agents are not happy about my actions. Ignoring the corpses of the lizard humanoids that they have yet to clean up, they begin to advance on me, but they stop when I wrap one of my hands around Konoa's throat. Konoa makes a gulping sound, but my scanners indicate that he is too afraid of what I

103

might do to him to act.

"Machine, what are you doing to Konoa?" Rozan asks. The hems of his robes are burnt black, likely from the fire breath of the lizard humanoids, and there is a bad gash on his left arm, although he appears to be well besides that. "Why are you holding him like you're taking him hostage?"

"I do not mean to cause anyone harm," I say, twisting Konoa's left arm behind his back as uncomfortably as possible. "But the fact is, I am not an agent of this 'Foundation' and I have no interest in staying here or helping you in whatever it is you are doing. As a law enforcer of Xeeon, I must return to Xeeo immediately to reconnect with the Database and inform my fellow officers of my status. I do not wish to spend an indefinite period of time locked away in that tiny room again."

"Why'd you take Konoa as a hostage, then?" says Rozan. He rubs his forehead in exasperation. "Do you have a screw loose or something?"

"None of my screws are loose," I say. "And while it normally goes against my programming to hold innocents hostage, I know you will not let me leave of my own free will even if I ask politely; hence, why I will let Konoa go only if I am allowed to leave freely."

"By Waran-Una's name," says Rozan. He shakes his head. "This is why I don't trust robots. They pull stuff like this at the last minute, completely out of the blue. Palos should have left you to be destroyed by Jornan back there."

"I am sorry you think I am not a good example of robots in general, but I do not care to be though of as a well-behaved robot right now," I say. "Now, if you would all move out of the way and let me leave this room, then I will let Konoa free without harming him, as I said before."

Scanners indicate that the agents before me—by my count, 40 in all—are confused and angry, though mostly angry. While most of their anger seems to stem from my taking Konoa hostage, I also believe they are worn out from battling and killing the lizard humanoids, which is probably contributing to their bad moods. Many of them wield swords or other weapons, which are covered in blood from the earlier battle.

But I do not care if they are angry, confused, or happy. What matters is whether they will agree to my offer. I do not intend to murder Konoa—my programming specifically forbids me from murdering innocents or individuals who do not pose a threat to my safety or the safety of others—but I will harm him if necessary. The only question is whether the agents will agree to my offer or not. I am not certain what I will do if they refuse, but I will figure it out if that happens.

Then Rozan chuckles. He gestures at his fellow agents, saying, "Lower your weapons, boys. I think this robot made a reasonable request."

"Rozan?" says Konoa. His voice trembles. "Why are you—"

"Because we don't *need* the robot around here anymore," says Rozan. He wipes some blood trickling from the corner of his mouth. "He can go and find his way back to Xeeo all on his own. No one will believe him if he tries to tell them about us; what's the harm?"

To say I am suspicious of Rozan's sudden change in attitude is an understatement. I do a quick scan to see if Rozan is lying, but his body does not display any of the typical symptoms of a liar.

For whatever reason, Rozan genuinely appears to want to let me go.

"What's the harm?" says Konoa. He grimaces, likely due to the pressure I am putting on his left arm. "Rozan, you of all people should know what the harm is in letting J997 go."

"All I know is that clickers like him can be ridiculously hard to stop, even with forty Foundation agents working together to take him down," says Rozan. "So why waste precious time keeping him here when we could use that same time figuring out what Reunification's next move will be?"

"What about the Head?" asks Konoa. "Did you speak with her about this?"

Rozan scowls. "Look, it doesn't matter. Rina, why don't you teleport our guest out of here? No need to delay, after all."

That is when I notice Rina, the witch from before. She is not standing with the other agents; instead, she is standing twelve feet to my right. She does not appear to have been in the battle at all, as I see no scars on her or wounds. Even her clothes appear to be in perfect condition, although I do not recall seeing her during the battle.

Before I can react, Rina raises her hand and snaps her fingers.

As soon as she does, I feel Konoa slip out of my fingers, while the world around me turns black for a split second.

The next moment, I find myself standing in the middle of a wintery, snowy landscape, with no sign of the Foundation or any sort of Delanian civilization for as far as my optics can see.

Chapter 7

Scanners indicate that the temperature of the environment around me is below 10 degrees. While I am not in danger of freezing thanks to my internal heating systems, it is still not good for me to be out here in this weather for a prolonged period of time.

Snow is falling from the sky; not very heavily, but my interior weather forecast system suggests that a heavy snowstorm is on its way here and that I should look for shelter right away. Although I may be a strong robot lacking the usual weaknesses of most organics, it will not be wise for me to stay out here in the middle of a blizzard. There is a high chance I will be frozen and buried in snow, and with the apparent lack of civilization for as far as my optics can see, there is no guarantee at all that anyone will find and dig me out of the snow, should that happen.

Where, exactly, have I ended up? Aside from the heavy snowfall everywhere, mountain peaks tower around me, and the ground is rocky and uneven under my feet. I appear to have landed in some kind of frozen mountains, possibly the

Winterlands, the coldest place on Dela. The pictures of the Winterlands in the mobile Database resemble what I am currently seeing, although there are no trees within my vision and there does not seem to be any sign of life at all.

I also wonder why Rina the witch teleported me out here in the middle of the Winterlands. Is the Foundation's Delanian branch located in the Winterlands? That is a possibility, as long-range teleportation is not easy for most wizards and witches to accomplish (according to the mobile Database's files on the subject, anyway). If so, then their headquarters is probably somewhere nearby, although with all of the snow piled everywhere, I cannot locate it even with my scanners.

But I do not need to. I am now free from that place. All I need to do now is find a nearby village or town whose inhabitants can point me in the direction of the nearest Portal to Xeeo and then I will hopefully be able to reestablish contact with the Database in a few days or weeks. According to the mobile Database, most of the Winterlands' settlements—including the large city of Delig— are located on the southern end of the mountains, where it is warmer and easier to live.

The problem is that I do not know my exact location, so I have no idea which way is south. Nor can I connect with any satellites in the sky above to aid me, as the Delanians do not use satellites and have forbidden several Xeeonite companies in the past from establishing satellites in Dela's orbit.

Then again, this may be for the best. If the Foundation's agents told me the truth earlier, then I am a wanted criminal in Dela. If I reconnect with civilization, then I run the risk of being arrested and possibly even destroyed. That is not an exaggeration;

ALLIANCE

I know how well the Knights of Se-Dela are respected, even outside of their home country, and so if everyone believes that I murdered them, then only the cruelest punishment awaits me, especially if I run into more Knights.

Nonetheless, I must go, because my only other alternative is to stay here and allow the snow to bury me. Logic dictates that it is better to risk being captured and executed as a criminal than it is to hide in these mountains from civilization. Besides, all of the information I have learned about the Foundation, Reunification, and the lizard humanoids needs to be uploaded to the Database right away, so I have no time to lose.

My best bet is to head for Delig and see if I can find any Xeeonite visitors there. The mobile Database's files say that Delig is a popular tourist destination for Xeeonites visitors due to the extreme lack of snow on that world. There is even a ski resort owned and operated by Mayor Xacron-Ah, the Mayor of Xeeon, which seems like a good destination for me to go to, because that is likely where I will find Xeeonite tourists who may be sympathetic to my plight.

As soon as I take a step forward, my sensors pick up an abrupt spike of skyras energy directly to my left. A woman wearing silver robes—the Head—appears at my side, scowling and glaring at me like I have offended her somehow. Her clothing does not appear to be very practical for this weather, but the cold barely seems to bother her.

"Come here," says the Head. She grabs my arm before I can respond. "We're going back. Right now."

She tugs on my arm and the Winterlands disappear around us as quickly as they appeared.

In the next instant, I find myself standing in their headquarters again, only this time, I am not in the Portal room. Instead, I am standing inside a room I have never been inside before.

It is a round room, with full bookshelves running along its perimeter. A large wooden table, inscribed with designs that resemble creatures like hawks and bulls, stands in the center of the room, around which many Foundation agents are seated. Among them are Konoa, Rozan, Nacina, and Rina (though not Lanresia; although as she is likely still healing from the attack on the Xeeonite branch, it is only logical for her not to be here).

The others turn to look at us when we teleport in, except for Rozan, who keeps his head facing the table. He is doodling on a blank piece of paper, as if in an attempt to appear busy, although even I can tell he only wants to avoid looking at me, though I do not know why.

The Head lets go of my arm and stomps over to the table. She takes her seat on a large silver chair—almost a throne—that elevates her slightly above the other agents. I stand where we teleported in, unsure where to go or what to do, as I do not see any empty seats for me to take.

The Head looks at Rozan, who is still resolutely doodling, but does not say anything at first. Nor do any of the other agents, who are trying as much as Rozan to avoid looking at their leader. It is a puzzling thing; after all, shouldn't the Head be pleased with them, considering how they all helped defend their headquarters from those lizard humanoids from before?

"Excuse me," I say, keeping my tone level and respectful. "I don't understand—"

The Head holds up one hand and I shut up. I do not want to

shut up, but she seems so angry that I do not think it would be wise or logical for me to go against her obvious commands. Better to wait and see what she is angry about before I do anything else.

"Rozan," says the Head, her tone short. She is glaring at him even worse than she glared at me earlier. "What do you have to say for yourself for ordering Rina to teleport J997 out of the headquarters and into the middle of the Winterlands like that? *Without* my permission or knowledge?"

Rozan still does not look up. As he continues to doodle away, he says, "It was just supposed to be a joke. He kept talking about how much he wanted to leave this place and go home, so I thought, why not show him why that's a stupid idea?"

"Did you even think about what would happen if Reunification found him?" asks the Head. She gestures at me with one of her hands. "Or if he got caught in that terrible blizzard that's coming this way? We would have lost him for good and someone else—like an agent of Reunification—might have found him instead."

"So?" says Rozan. He sounds much less confident than he normally does, despite not making any eye contact with the Head. "He's just a stupid robot. It's not like he's a special snowflake or whatever."

"As long as J997 knows as much about us as he does, he cannot leave this place," says the Head. "Even teleporting him into the middle of nowhere for a stupid 'lesson' is dangerous. We must always know where he is at all times, because if Reunification were to get him, they could take his knowledge of us and use it against us."

To me, that seems like a strange thing to say, because I don't know very much about the Foundation at all. Even if Reunification found me and took my knowledge, I doubt they would gain much from it.

But I say nothing, because I am more interested in listening to the conversation at hand in case they say anything important.

"But we *did* know where he was," says Rozan. His doodles look more like scribbles, now that I zoom in with my optics. "You found him and brought him back here easily. I don't see what the big deal is."

"I only found out about your numbskull idea when Konoa told me about it," says the Head, gesturing at Konoa as she speaks. "By that time, only a few minutes had elapsed between Rina teleporting J997 outside and the time I was informed of this, but in our world, a few minutes can mean the difference between life and death. You should know this."

Rozan finally looks up, meeting the Head's angry eyes. He has also stopped doodling and scribbling, although he still holds the pencil in his oversized dwarf fist. "I *do* know that. I was just so annoyed by the dumb machine that I didn't think it'd matter. And I think I deserve a little more recognition for how I helped fight off those damn lizard monsters."

"Yes, I appreciate the help, but that does not change the irresponsibility of your actions," says the Head. "You have always been headstrong and foolish, Rozan, but in all of the years I've known you, this has to be the dumbest thing you have ever done."

Rozan drops his pencil on the table without looking away from the Head. He stands up. "All right. I messed up. What are you going to do now? Throw me in the dungeons?"

It is hard for me to tell if Rozan is joking or being serious about the dungeons, although his sarcastic tone seems to indicate he is joking. The other agents all appear embarrassed, especially Nacina, who is looking down at her lap rather than at the table.

The Head leans back in her chair, but she looks more troubled than relaxed. "No. Right now, I do not have any time to punish you. With the loss of the Xeeonite branch and the dozens of agents here who were badly injured in that earlier assault, we need every able-bodied agent we can get to defend our base."

Rozan's shoulders slump, like he had hoped she wouldn't say that. He then sits back down on his chair, folding his arms over his chest, although he does not do or say anything else. The other agents still do not look at him, even though the Head does not appear to be angry at him anymore.

The Head looks at the other agents. "All right. Now that we have that out of the way, I think it's time for us to discuss our next plan of action before Reunification strikes again."

Before the agents can respond, I hold up my hand and say, "Excuse me, but I do not understand why I am here. I am not a member of the Foundation, so why are you including me in this group meeting?"

"As I said, we need to keep you in our sight at all times," says the Head. "Besides, we already know that you can escape from wherever we put you. You proved that earlier today, when you broke out of that room earlier and assaulted some of our agents. So I've decided to keep an eye on you myself."

"I see," I say. I look around the room and spot a door on the other side of the table, to the right of the Head's chair. "Is that door the only way in and out of here?"

"Yes," says the Head. "But don't try to leave. The door's locked with skyras energy, so even you couldn't break it down if you tried."

I have no intention whatsoever of trying to escape at the moment, because it is clear to me that escape from this place is almost completely impossible. I still want to escape, of course, but for now that is outside of my abilities. I will keep an optic lit, however, for an opportunity to escape to show itself to me later on.

"But the robot will get to listen to our plans," says Rozan, tossing a glare at me. "And what if he *does* escape and reconnect with the Database? Or gets captured by Reunification, like you just berated me about?"

"Rozan, I do not want to hear another word from you for the duration of this meeting," says the Head, without even looking at him. "Besides, you already risked blowing our cover when you had Rina here teleport J997 outside. I find your worry about his connecting with the Database to be quite hypocritical; in any case, he will not escape, so it's not a big worry for me at the moment."

Rozan does not respond to that. He simply crosses his arms even more tightly around his body and refuses to look at anyone. Not even Nacina looks at him now, which is strange because Nacina and Rozan always seemed like friends to me. Perhaps they are not as close as they appear or maybe Nacina does not want to anger the Head.

In either case, the Head resumes speaking. "Anyway, it is quite clear at this point that Reunification not only sent those lizard beasts after us, but also destroyed the Xeeonite branch.

114

That means they must be moving closer to completing their Mission."

"By Waran-Una's name," says Konoa, covering his mouth with one of his hands. "But how can that be? I thought our spies had reported that Reunification was still far from achieving their goal."

"At this point, I don't know," says the Head. "None of us do. But I can think of no other reason for why they would go to the trouble of attacking our Xeeonite branch unless they were entering the final stages of their plan."

"So they're trying to take out all possible opposition in order to complete the final stages of the Mission without delay?" says Nacina. She rubs her hands together anxiously. "How did they even find the headquarters of the Xeeonite branch? I thought we kept the locations of our bases a secret from outsiders."

"That is another troubling mystery," says the Head. She brushes her blonde hair out of her eyes. "But considering we have not heard back from any of our spies, I think we must face the very real possibility that one of our spies has either turned or else was discovered and forced to reveal all he knows to the enemy."

"I don't like either of those two options much," says Konoa. "Have we tried communicating with any of our spies?"

"I ordered some of our elves to contact them," says the Head. She grimaces. "There was no answer. Right now, we must assume they were discovered and tortured for their knowledge about us, which means that they are dead, in all likelihood."

"Horrid," says Rina, which is the first time I have ever heard her speak. She is shaking her head, a frown on her aged features. "But logical, from Reunification's point of view."

"Indeed it is, Rina," says the Head. "And I think it is safe for us to assume that Reunification not only knows the location of the Xeeonite headquarters, but also the location of this base."

She gestures at the room we are in, although I understand that she is referring to the headquarters as a whole.

"Then we must reinforce the defenses," says Konoa, slamming one fist on the table. "We must find as many able-bodied agents as possible and set them up to guard all of the entrances and exits. We must also shut down all Portals between Dela and Xeeo in this base so that Reunification does not attempt to invade us directly again."

"Already done," says the Head. "That is what I was doing while you fought off that assault from the lizard creatures. Every Portal that links this base to the Xeeonite one has been shut off and destroyed for good measure, so it's impossible for them to invade us that way."

Although I know I am not technically part of this discussion, hearing the Head mention destroying those Portals reminds me of a joke I read about in *Secrets of Humor*.

So I step forward and say, "Then I guess those Reunification agents will need to be portal monkeys in order to get here. Right, fellows?"

The Head and the Foundation agents turn as one to look at me. I do not understand the lack of understanding on their faces, as this joke makes perfect sense to me.

"Don't you understand the joke?" I say. "It's a reference to portal monkeys, the only organic creatures on Dela and Xeeo that can use portals naturally. The joke is that the only way these Reunification people could get here now is if they were portal monkeys. Get it?"

Their facial expressions do not change at all, except for Rozan, who lowers his face into his hands and mutters something that my audio receptors pick up as, "And he tells jokes, too. Bad ones. Why me?"

"Anyway," says the Head, drawing the attention of the agents back to her. "The point is that it is extremely unlikely that Reunification will attempt another invasion of the base, now that they have no way of transporting large groups of those monstrosities across directly into here."

"That's a relief," says Nacina with a sigh. Then she scratches the side of her face. "But what about the exterior? I agree with Konoa that we must shore up our defenses before they attempt to attack us that way."

"I agree with both of you," says the Head. "While Reunification's moves are often unpredictable, we can at least ensure that our defenses are capable of handling whatever they will try to throw at us."

"Then what are we waiting for?" says Konoa. He puts his hands on the arms of his chair, like he is ready to stand up. "I shall go and find as many able-bodied agents as I can and send them to protect the entrances."

"An excellent idea," says the Head. She gestures toward the door behind her. "Go. Reunification moves fast, so we must move faster if we are going to stay on top of them and predict their every move before they make it."

Konoa nods and stands up from his chair. He then dashes around the table toward the door, which he opens and disappears through. He then slams the door shut, which seems unnecessary to me, although I say nothing about it.

"What about us, ma'am?" says Nacina, gesturing at herself, Rina, and Rozan. "Should we go and help Konoa recruit as many able-bodied agents as possible?"

"No," says the Head, shaking her head. "I have different plans for you three. Konoa can do this job on his own."

"Then what do you want us to do?" says Rozan, who apparently is unable to stay silent. "Sit here and be quiet little agents, like children told to sit here by their mommy?"

"Of course not," says the Head. "Rina, I need you to go and ensure that all of the witches and wizards have their skyras rings and are ready to use them at a moment's notice."

Rina nods, and the next instant she's gone, leaving behind no sign at all that she had been sitting there moments ago. I do not even sense her presence anymore, though I suspect that is due to the Head's own overwhelming skyras energy levels completely eclipsing the levels of everyone else.

"As for you two, go and help prepare the bodies of the deceased agents for the mass burial," says the Head. "We will not be able to give them a proper burial at the moment due to the current situation, but at least make sure that all of the bodies are gathered up, taken to the morgue, and identified so we know exactly who we lost."

"Yes, ma'am," says Nacina as she stands up. "Come on, Rozan."

Rozan does not appear happy about this, but he does stand up and walk with Nacina to the door. Once they are gone, it is now just the Head and me, who is still sitting on her chair with her head lowered, as if she is thinking.

I do not want to stand around here and do nothing, even though boredom is not as much of a problem for me as it is for organics. But I cannot leave, either, as the Head has already said that she wants to keep me here, where she can keep an eye on me.

But perhaps this is not as bad as it appears. By speaking with the Head, I might be able to learn more about the Foundation and Reunification. If I cannot leave this place, then I can at least learn more about these two organizations so I can understand better what is going on here, and possibly collect information for the Database once I return to Xeeo. Then again, the Head doesn't look like she is in the mood to tell me anything.

Without warning, the Head raises her head and looks at me with stern eyes. She seems displeased with me, although why, I do not know. After all, I have not done anything to bother her. Maybe I unintentionally offended her somehow.

Then the Head says, "J997, what do you think about this recent series of events?"

I do not know why she asks that question. I doubt she sincerely wants to know my opinion, considering how she does not know me well at all, but if I refuse to answer her question, then I might anger her. If I actually knew her or had information on her in the mobile Database, it would be a lot easier to know what to say.

Deciding that answering her question is better than not, I say, "It is all very confusing. When I came to Dela a couple of days ago, I did not think I would end up in a place like this. I thought I would only need to help the Knights of Se-Dela arrest Jornan ah Kona and bring her before the court of law to be judged for her crimes."

119

"I understand," says the Head. "Even I do not completely understand what is going on here. Reunification has rarely directly attacked us like this. It disturbs me more than I have been disturbed in many years. It makes me question myself."

As the Head speaks, I do a brief scan of her body, something I have not been able to do thanks to the hurried-ness of the last few hours, in order to understand her biology better. She appears human on the surface, but the immense amount of skyras energy she radiates, as well as her oddly-swollen back, make me doubt that she is in any way mortal.

But despite my best efforts, my scan comes up incomplete. Apparently my scanner is unable to tell me anything about her, aside from her skyras energy levels. Perhaps she has some kind of device she is using to block my scanner or maybe it is the skyras energy itself blocking my scan.

"I know you just attempted to scan me, J997," says the Head, snapping me out of my thoughts. "I can tell. You robots are not very hard to figure out."

"I only scanned you to find out what you are," I say; there is no reason for me to lie, so I do not. "You appear human, but at the same time, different."

"I know how unusual I am," says the Head. "But I won't let you find out what I am just yet. That is information you do not need to know at the moment, especially because not even my agents know my true nature."

"Are you a genetically-modified human?" I ask. "Or did you use Delanian magic to change you?"

The Head shakes her head. "Neither, but that is where I will leave it for now. You know how tight-lipped we Foundation agents are about our secrets."

"I know," I say. "But I still do not like not knowing what you are. Ignorance has caused more harm in the two worlds than anything else in the world."

"I would say that well-intentioned extremism has caused more harm than anything ignorance has ever done," says the Head. "But I am not in a mood to discuss complicated and lengthy philosophical issues with you. I have something more important for you to do. Would you like to know what that is?"

"Of course," I say. "Ever since you sent out your agents, I have wondered why you kept me here. Do you have a mission for me to accomplish?"

"No," says the Head, shaking her head. "As you are not an agent of the Foundation, I have no missions for you to take. Instead, I am going to have you help me in other ways."

I fold my arms over my chest. "Other ways? What might those 'other ways' be?"

The Head chuckles, which makes no sense to me, because I did not make any jokes this time. "You remind me of another robot I once knew years ago. I was just chuckling at the resemblance between you and him. And I thank you for it, because it has been a long time since I've been able to chuckle about anything."

I still do not see what is so humorous about any similarities between me and this other robot she once knew, but I decide not to ask. On the other hand, if I can find out what is so humorous about it, then maybe that will help me tell better jokes.

Before I can ask for further clarification, the Head says, "Now I know I said I wanted to keep you here in the base so that you do not compromise our secrecy, but there are still ways you can help us. Of course, I won't tell you too much detail about these ways, seeing as you are not an agent, but I will give you just enough information to make you useful."

"I dislike going into any situation without complete knowledge of it," I say. "It is unwise to enter a situation without knowing all of the facts."

The Head frowns. "I expected that, though I must say, the robot I once knew would have agreed without question. I suppose the two of you are not quite the same after all."

"I will consider helping you if you tell me what you need or want me to do," I say. "As it is, you have been speaking very vaguely about all of it. This makes me suspect that you want me to do something that is illegal and unlawful."

"It is nothing of the sort," says the Head. "While the Foundation does operate outside of the law to achieve our goals, what I am going to have you do is perfectly legal under Delanian and Xeeonite laws."

"Are you certain of that?" I ask. "You do not seem like a lawyer to me."

"I am certain of it," says the Head, nodding. "Now, do you want to hear my offer or not?"

"Very well," I say. "I am listening."

The Head laces her fingers together, a thoughtful look on her face. She appears to be thinking about what to say to me, which means she is deciding what information to share with me and what not to. If I had telepathy, I would be able to read her mind, but J bots were not designed with the ability to read non-mechanical minds, so I must wait for her to speak in order to find out what she is thinking.

Then she looks at me with a more focused look and says, "All right. I want you to go down and help the other agents examine the corpses of the lizard creatures that attacked earlier. You can use your scanning technology to help us better understand how these creatures are put together and search for any weaknesses in them that we may be unaware of."

That sounds like a simple, reasonable request. I, too, am interested in learning more about these creatures, which, based on the evidence I have gathered so far, are not natural creatures from Dela or Xeeo. Mostly, I want to find out more about them so I can put their information in the Database when I return to Xeeo in order that the Database will continue to be the most perfect and up-to-date record of every species on both worlds.

On the other hand, the Head has already said that she is not going to give me all of the information about the job she wants me to do. That means she has her own hidden agenda for why she wants me to examine these creatures and understand their genetic makeup, although what it is I do not know. The most likely explanation is that she wants to know more about them so the Foundation can fight them more effectively in the future; however, she likely has other reasons for doing this, too, and perhaps not noble or good-intentioned reasons, either.

I detest helping people who refuse to share their true intentions with me, but the only other alternative, it seems to me, is to remain here as a virtual prisoner while the Foundation battles against the mysterious Reunification organization. At least if I accept her offer I stand a chance of learning information that will help to complete the Database's records, if nothing else.

So I nod and say, "All right. I will do as you ask. I will not ask you further about why you want me to do it, but I will do it nonetheless."

"That is good to hear," says the Head. "Your cooperation is much appreciated. Now, it's time to send you to the—"

The Head ceases speaking. She looks around, like she thinks someone might be eavesdropping on our conversation, although my optics and sensors alike confirm that we are the only two beings in this room.

"Head?" I say. "What is the problem? Did you hear something? If so, what was it?"

The Head stands up from her chair with a serious look on her face. She looks this way and that, but again I do not see what she thinks she sees or hears. I wonder if this is some sort of test on her part, although what she is testing me on, I do not know.

Finally, however, the Head stops looking around and then looks at me. A frown crosses her thin lips and her skin seems unusually pale, as though she is afraid of something.

"What?" I say. "I do not know what you think you hear, but you and I are the only two beings in this room."

"I know we are alone in this room," says the Head, although her voice is almost a whisper now. "Do you sense that?"

I check my skyras sensors, but aside from the Head's unusually large skyras levels, I sense nothing out of the ordinary.

"No," I say. "What do you sense?"

The Head gulps. She jumps off her chair, lands on the ground gracefully, and then stands up.

She looks at me again, only this time, she says, "I sense an army about to batter down the doors of this very base. And if we are not fast, then they *will* succeed, and we will be destroyed."

Chapter 8

Before I can ask what army she is referring to, the Head says, "You stay here. I don't want to lose you in the battle that is probably already starting below."

"Hold on," I say, holding out a hand toward her. "What is this army that you speak of? Is it from Reunification? More of those lizard creatures, perhaps?"

"Probably," says the Head. She puts one hand on her forehead and frowns. "But I can't tell for certain. If you could feel it yourself, then you would understand why I want you to stay here. This army is too big and powerful to risk losing you to. That is why you must stay here."

"But I am a J bot," I say. "I can fight and take care of myself. My energy level is only at seventy-six percent now, after all, and I am still in good shape from the previous fight."

"What about that hole in your chest?" says the Head, pointing at my chest. "The one that looks like one of those lizard creatures from earlier made it?"

I look down at my chest. The hole is still there and still needs to be looked at by a certified J bot technician, but I completely forgot about it until now.

"I will be fine," I say, covering my hole with my hand. "It is not a debilitating wound; it is what you organics might call a 'flesh wound,' if I had flesh. I can still move and fight without trouble."

"No," says the Head. "Stay here. If the battle is successful, then I will be back shortly. Right now, I need to rally the surviving agents into whatever fighting force I can gather."

In the blinking of an optic, the Head is gone, leaving me all alone in this room. Even so, I can still sense her skyras level, which is intriguing because she should probably be out of my range by now. Of course, her aura is fainter now, but the fact that I can feel it at all means that she is even stronger than my sensors indicate (although that could be because the Foundation agents altered my skyras sensors, of course).

I am now the only entity left in this room. I consider simply standing here and waiting for the Head's return, or the return of one of the other Foundation agents, but then I decide that this is the perfect opportunity to attempt to make an escape.

With no one to stop me, I dash over to the door and attempt to open it. Unfortunately, I soon discover that the door is still locked with skyras energy, even after I punch it as hard as I can, which fails to even create a dent in the door. The door looks normal, but the skyras energy protecting it must be reinforcing its strength.

I turn around, hoping to find another way out of here that I might have missed earlier. That seems doubtful, but I am aware that the Foundation has many secrets and I would not put it past them to have secret doors or rooms hidden in their base.

Especially in this place, which appears to be an important meeting room, which would undoubtedly require a secret exit for members to escape through in the event of an attack like this one.

The only question is, how do I find these secret passageways, if they actually exist? I have no x-ray vision, after all, nor am I familiar enough with Delanian architecture to search for the telltale signs of hidden passages. The mobile Database has few articles on the subject, though that does not surprise me, seeing as the mobile Database does not contain articles on every obscure subject in the two worlds.

Therefore, if I am going to find out how to escape this place (and by this place, I do not mean merely this room, but the base in general, because I have no reason to stay around here any longer), then I must search by hand. That will take time, no doubt, but right now all I have is time, so it is not much of an issue for me.

I begin walking along the room's perimeter, my eyes scanning the bookshelves that curve with the room's walls. I do not recognize the titles of any of these books—*Prophecy's End, Man of My Own Heart, The Tiller's Tale, Rise and Fall of the Old Gods*—but they appear to be fiction titles, oddly enough. I compare their titles to the list of Delanian novels in the mobile Database, but I find no match for any of these titles. This makes me wonder just how far these Foundation agents are willing to go to keep their secrecy if even their own books apparently do not exist.

In any case, none of the book titles catch my interest or appear highly unusual, aside from not existing within the mobile Database. I consider the possibility that some of these books may be fakes, with their true nature being switches or levers used to open secret passageways, but there are so many books that I doubt it is worth my time to try each and every one in my attempt to find the fake ones.

Another thing I notice about these books is how old they appear. Their spines are worn and aged, their titles barely legible even to my sharp optics. I find it strange how the Head has apparently decided to keep all of these big, thick tomes rather than digitize them all and put them on a portable computer. I suppose it is the general Delanian aversion to Xeeonite technology at work here, which makes me wonder if the Head is a Delanian native herself.

That is when I notice a single piece of paper stuck between two particularly thick books. I almost miss it because it is so thin, but one of its corners pokes out, which makes me stop and reach for it to see if it might help me find a way out of here. I gently tug the paper out of the place between the two books and look down at it out of curiosity.

The paper is old and crinkly, with one of its corners bitten off, probably by some kind of rodent, although I am unable to identify what species of rodent exactly due to the odd shape of the bite mark. In addition, there is a strange, dried green liquid that looks like dried blood, although my scanner fails to match the green liquid with any known Delanian or Xeeonite species recorded in the mobile Database.

On the paper itself is an old, faded drawing. The drawing is so faded that even I, with my superior optics, am unable to make out all of its details in full. A quick scan reveals that its paint—like the green blood above—has no match in the mobile Database, so I cannot trace its paint to its source.

From what I can make out of the drawing itself, it shows a poorly-drawn young human female, not older than eight-years-old, sitting on a blanket in the middle of a green field, with curly blonde hair (although I do not know if that color is indeed green or if it is simply faded due to its age). Sitting next to the young human female is a robot similar in size, with two big lantern-like red eyes and what appears to be a bandanna tied around its neck. And on the robot's right is a young human male, close in age to the girl, with bright blue eyes.

Below the young human female, her robot friend, and the young human male are some illegible words, although even if they were legible, I doubt I would be able to read them. Their shapes do not resemble the written form of any Delanian or Xeeonite language that the mobile Database has records on.

This drawing only brings more questions to mind. Why does the Head apparently own this old drawing? Who does it depict? It certainly does not resemble the great art of the Delanian Masters, a group of painters known throughout the two worlds for their artistic mastery. Why then does she have it here, stuck in between two large books? And just who are these individuals depicted on it?

I consider keeping the drawing, as the paper and ink used to make the drawing have their own unique properties that deserve further investigation, but then I realize that taking this drawing would be theft. Seeing as I am not a thief, I decide to replace the drawing where I found it, although before I do that I snap a picture of it to keep in my memory so I can examine it in more detail later, when I have time to do so.

After making sure that the drawing is back where I found it, I resume walking around the perimeter of the room, my optics scanning the books as I do so. I still see no sign of any secret passages or doorways, but that does not mean there are not any there. It just means that I have to search harder.

I walk past bookshelf after bookshelf, my optics scanning each book as I pass. Not individually, as I am walking too fast to do that, but in groups, which is much quicker.

But after another minute or two of walking, I find myself back at the only door to this room, exactly where I started not long ago. I am now no closer to discovering a way out of here than I was before.

I almost decide to give up and wait until someone—perhaps the Head, maybe another Foundation agent—comes up to check up on me. But then I notice the table that the Head and those other agents had been sitting around earlier and wonder if I might be able to find a secret passageway there.

I walk up to the table and look down on it. A scan of the table tells me that it is made of Delanian elvish wood, which takes me aback slightly, because I was certain that my scan would tell me that this table is made of some kind of unidentifiable wood. Perhaps not everything about this Foundation is a secret or shrouded in mystery.

The surface of the table is carved with images of creatures that resemble hawks and bulls, as I noticed earlier. Yet I notice significant differences from actual hawks and bulls, such as one carving, which features a hawk with burning feathers and wings, and a carving of a bull that appears to have swords for horns. I know of no creatures on Dela or Xeeo that resemble those, which makes me wonder if these are simply the products of an artist's imagination or if they are stylized carvings of real animals.

In any case, it does not matter. What I need to do is search this table for any secret buttons or switches that might reveal a secret passageway to me. It is my last chance; if this table does not lead to any secret passages, then I will truly be stuck in this room until the Head or someone else returns.

So, starting at the Head's silver chair, I carefully run my fingers along the underside of the table, using the sensors on my fingertips to feel for any bumps or other unusual protrusions that might indicate the presence of a button of some sort. The wood is smooth so far, but I keep feeling nonetheless.

I make my way around the table slowly in order to avoid missing anything. At the same time, I keep my audio receptors open so I can hear anyone coming to get me on the other side of the door. My audio receptors, however, pick up nothing except the occasional rumbling in the floor, which is probably the result of the fighting against that army that the Head mentioned.

Soon, I find myself back at the Head's silver chair again, having found no hidden buttons whatsoever. Removing my hands from under the table, I step back and look at my surroundings once more, although it is hard for me to resume my search for another possible way out when I have effectively exhausted all possible candidates.

Maybe I really do have to wait here until someone comes for me. The more I stand here and think about it, the more likely that seems. How long I will have to wait, I do not know, as it depends entirely on how effective the Foundation agents are at fighting off that army.

I lean against the Head's chair, not because I am tired, but because I have nothing better to do and I dislike simply standing in one place. Leaning on the chair will hopefully take off some of the pressure on my joints, although I doubt they need it, seeing as my joints are state-of-the-art and are in excellent condition at the moment.

I consider perhaps taking down some of those books and reading them in order to pass the time when the sensors on my fingertips discover something. I look at the arm of the Head's chair, but it appears as smooth as ever to me, even though I am certain that my sensors picked up something unusual there.

I run my fingertips along the chair's left arm and discover, much to my astonishment, a panel that can be pressed down. It is completely flat with the rest of the arm, making it invisible to the naked eye, but applying even the gentlest of pressure reveals its presence right away.

Could this be the entrance to the secret passageway I have been looking for? Maybe. It is worth trying; at any rate, I doubt it will do anything terrible to me.

So I press down on the panel, though gently in order to avoid breaking it.

As soon as I push it down all the way, the chair moves backwards without warning. I step back, even though it does not appear hostile or dangerous, and watch as the chair slides backwards across the floor. Once it stops, I look at what it reveals.

The removal of the chair reveals a square hole—same width as the chair's base—where the chair had been a moment before. This hole has a ladder leading down into the darkness. I switch to night vision to allow me to see down into the dark hole, but the hole is so deep that I cannot see its bottom even with my night vision active.

I dislike going down into places that are too dark for me to see in even with my night vision; I have no choice, however, but to climb down this ladder and find out what is below. There may or may not be a dead end, but the only way I can find out for certain is by going down there myself.

As I suspected, the hole is quite deep. Even though I have been climbing down it for five minutes now, I still cannot see the bottom even when I look down. Furthermore, when I descended into the hole, the chair slid back into place above me. While it may be possible for me to open it again, there is a good possibility that it cannot be opened except from the outside, which means I must continue climbing down regardless of the danger that awaits.

While I climb down, I still do not hear any sounds from the outside. I wonder how the battle against the invading army is going. Is the Foundation winning or is Reunification winning? What will happen if one of them defeats the other?

I find that I do not particularly care. While Reunification has harmed me in worse ways than the Foundation, my trust for the Foundation is still quite limited. They have continually refused to tell me all of the facts; I do not even know why they are fighting Reunification or what they hope to achieve by doing so. It makes no sense to me to ally with them when they have not trusted me at all, as if I am a child that cannot be trusted. I'd rather take my chance with the Delanian public that thinks I am a murderer than stay with this Foundation that does not trust me in the least.

Scanners indicate that the temperature is gradually lowering the further down I climb. There must not be any central heating down here, which supports my earlier belief that this place is supposed to be a secret. I make sure my own internal heating systems are keeping my body at a warm temperature, however, because I have no interest in freezing down here.

After a couple of minutes of climbing, I finally see the bottom of the shaft, and in another minute, I rest my feet on the floor. It is made of old, cracked concrete, which surprises me because Delanians do not use concrete often in the construction of their buildings. Then again, the agents who make up the Foundation hardly seem like typical Delanians to me.

I turn around and see a long hallway stretching down quite a ways. A corner at the end of the hall turns out of my sight, but my sensors do not indicate any living creatures are down here. I appear to be completely alone in this shaft, but appearances can be deceiving, so I move forward cautiously, prepared to fight in case something tries to take me by surprise.

This tunnel is quite plain, perhaps because it is only meant to be used as an emergency escape route. Still, Delanian architecture tends to place a heavy emphasis on symbols and carvings in their buildings, though again, the Foundation probably does not care about that sort of thing due to their mysterious nature.

Although I walk cautiously, I also walk quickly, making my way to the end of the hall as quickly as possible. After all, my sensors already show me that I am alone down here, and with no idea about the progress of the battle above, I cannot waste time in escaping. Whether the Foundation wins or Reunification wins, I must escape and return to Xeeo, where I will be safe at last.

When I turn the corner, I discover a closed metal door a few feet away from me. It is the only exit I can see, so I walk toward it without hesitation. Before opening the door, however, I scan it quickly. When the scan reveals nothing out of the ordinary about this door, I grab the handle and pull it open.

As soon as I do, I am assaulted by a blast of cold wind and snow, which briefly obscures my optics before I wipe it off. I then stick my head outside to look at the environment I am about to walk into.

It appears that I have emerged into the Winterlands, because I see snow everywhere, violently whirling about in the air and making it impossible to see anything except a wall of white. The sky is dark, partly thanks to the heavy cloud cover, but also due to the fact that the sun appears to be setting. My sensors indicate that the temperature is dropping even faster out here than it is inside, which makes me pull my head back in and close the door shut.

This is not good. Walking out into this blizzard will freeze me in my tracks, because even my internal heating systems are not enough to combat -20 degree (and constantly lowering) temperatures, at least for very long. There is a high probability that I will end up freezing out there and being buried underneath tons of snow, perhaps forever, unless the Foundation wins this battle and rescues me.

But what else am I supposed to do? I suppose I can wait in here until the storm dies down, but the mobile Database's files say that Winterlands blizzards can last for weeks at a time. I do not have weeks to wait around until this storm lasts; not even the battle between the Foundation and Reunification will last that long.

Logically, I have only one choice, which is to take my

chances with the blizzard outside and hope I can find a cave or some place else to wait out the storm. Then I can figure out where to go from there.

So, preparing myself for the task ahead, I raise my internal body temperature up as high as I can without burning or melting my interior, and then grab the handle. I pull the door open and immediately dash outside into the blizzard.

Visibility is zero out here. As I run, my optics can see nothing except the white snow that is swirling in the air and falling like an avalanche. My audio receptors hear nothing except the howling of the wind, which makes it impossible to hear anything else that might be nearby.

Not only that, but the snow is quite deep already. With every step I take, I sink up to my knees, which always requires a great effort from me to pull my legs out of. This slows my progress considerably more than I like, although I press forward nonetheless, occasionally using the jets in my feet to melt the snow. I try not to do that much in order to conserve my fuel.

I almost consider flying through this mess, but then realize that flying through an unknown territory with zero visibility is an idiotic move. It is better to keep walking forward with both of my feet on the ground than it is to fly and possibly crash into a normally easily avoidable rock wall or mountain peak.

As for my joints, sensors indicate that snow is starting to find its way into them. My internal heating system melts the snow, of course, but it is only a matter of time before I am frozen entirely and buried underneath the tons of snow pouring from the sky above. I must find shelter quickly.

But I cannot spot any caves or anywhere else for me to wait out the storm. The snow in the air and the darkness of the area makes it practically impossible for me to see my hands in front of my face, much less anything else. Maybe it would have been better for me to wait back inside the base, but there is no way I can find my way back there in this weather. I must instead push forward and hope that I do not walk into something dangerous. Even my sensors are unable to show what is ahead of me, mostly because the howling wind and thick snow blocks it.

And then, when I take another step forward, my foot does not find any ground and I fall forward over the edge of a cliff despite my best efforts to catch myself. As I fall head over heels, the snow swirls around me and my sensors are unable to tell the difference between up and down and which direction I am falling in.

I do not scream, nor do I feel any fear; instead, I activate my rocket boosters in an effort to cushion my landing. I then shoot through the air and slam face-first into a solid rock wall that I cannot see in the snow.

The impact of the blow makes me bounce off the wall, causing me to fall backwards through the air again. System scanners indicate my optics were slightly damaged in the collision with the wall, but I have no way to repair them. I instead activate my boosters again, deciding to focus on repairing my optics as soon as I leave these mountains.

This time, I adjust the strength of the boosters so I do not go flying uncontrollably through the air again. I try to float in the air, try to lower myself to the ground as carefully as possible, but the air and the snowy conditions make this difficult. The wind is blowing at 35 miles per hour, while the poor visibility makes it impossible for me to tell with any accuracy how far I am above the ground.

As a result, an unusually strong gust of wind knocks me over and I find myself falling again. This time, I have no time to activate my boosters again because I land hard on a thick pile of snow. The impact, while harsh, is not as bad as it would have been if I had not used my boosters to break my fall or if I had fallen on the earth.

Even so, system warnings indicate that my left leg has been damaged by the fall. It is still operational and should continue to support my weight, but it would be smart for me to have a qualified J bot technician look it over and make any adjustments as necessary.

But there are no qualified J bot technicians nearby, aside from Konoa, and he is nowhere near here. I will have to avoid putting too much stress on it until I can have a technician repair it.

I rise to my feet and look around at the area I have fallen into. It appears I have fallen into some sort of canyon or gorge, albeit not a wide one, because the wind is not blowing fiercely down here and the snow is not blowing in my face. It is still extremely cold, but at least my visibility is no longer as poor as it once was.

Above, I can see the snow swirling through the air and hear the howling winds. I can fly up there if I want, but I decide that it makes more sense to stay down here and wait out the storm rather than fly back up into that blizzard. While staying in one place might make it easier for the Foundation or Reunification to find me, I doubt any of them are planning on searching for me in this storm. Most likely, they will leave me alone for now, although I must still find shelter because even down here, the snow is terrible.

That is when I spot a large cave mouth on the opposite side of the canyon. An overhanging rock above the cave mouth appears to keep out most of the snow, so I decide to make that place my temporary shelter until the storm passes.

I make my way over to the cave without delay, as the snow down here is not nearly as deep as the snow above. Although it is slightly slippery, I manage to keep my balance and avoid falling over on my way over to the cave mouth.

Ducking to avoid scraping my head against the overhanging rock, I step into the cave. As soon as I do, the howling wind outside becomes muted, although the temperature drops even lower in here, most likely due to its small interior keeping the cold air in.

Before I go in any deeper, I do a brief scan of the cave. While it appears uninhabited, I am not in any mood to stumble upon some dangerous animal in here that will attack me for invading its territory.

Scan complete. Results: There are no living creatures in here at the moment, although there are the unidentifiable bones of some deceased creature—perhaps a dwarf, based on their thickness, although they are so old and incomplete that it is hard to tell—toward the back. The scan also reports dried blood stains on the ceiling and back walls, but again, I do not know what the blood may have belonged to because it is too old to determine its original species.

But aside from the bones and the blood, this cave shows no signs of being the home of any sort of creature. Therefore, it is safe to use it as shelter until the blizzard passes.

I walk to the back of the cave, as far from the howling wind and swirling snow outside as possible, and then turn and sit against the back wall. Energy levels are at sixty-nine percent at this point, which is a good energy level, although it is a reminder that I will need to return to Xeeo as soon as possible if I do not want to run out of power here in the middle of nowhere.

Yet I cannot continue my journey with the snow whirling around outside. Instead, I decide to go into sleep mode in order to conserve energy. I doubt anything will assault me here, after all, seeing as nothing lives in this case. I can also set up my heating systems to keep operating while I rest so my joints do not freeze due to lack of movement as I rest.

Still, I decide to set a definite time for me to wake up from sleep mode. Mobile Database records tell me that Winterlands blizzards can last up to three days, but sometimes can be as short as eight hours, so I decide to set my alarm for eight hours. If the blizzard is still raging even after that time, then I can simply go back to sleep.

Entering sleep mode in five ... four ... three ... two ... one ...

When I awaken, I notice that my interior alarm still has at least an hour left on it. That makes me wonder why I have left sleep mode when I notice something pale-skinned and winged standing over me, raising its claws above its head like it is about to attack me.

Without waiting, I raise my right hand and fire twin finger lightning bolts at the creature. It vanishes into the shadows before my lightning bolts can hit it, however, and then reappears several feet away, hissing and growling at me like an angry bear.

I rise to my feet and observe the creature as it hisses at me. As I noted before, it is pale and winged, but also humanoid, with crimson eyes and stained red lips. In addition, my scan picks up traces of snow bear blood on its lips, which confirms this creature's identity: It is an arctic vampire.

According to the mobile Database, arctic vampires are vampires that live primarily in the Delanian Winterlands and other cold climates. Due to their viciousness toward outsiders, there is not much information on their language, customs, or social structures, although it is known that they suck blood and never show mercy to their prey. It is not known exactly how they procreate, either, because no infant or youthful arctic vampires have ever been seen before.

This is the first time I have seen an arctic vampire in person. Its movements are jerky and unnatural, which makes it seem more robotic than organic, although I have seen robots with more life in them than this creature. Still, I am not fooled; the mobile Database's records state that arctic vampires are known to be strong enough to tear apart robots with metalligick plating. Therefore, I cannot let my guard down around this creature, no matter how pathetic or strange it may look.

And it does look as though it has not eaten in quite a while. Its body is thin and boney and its pale skin makes it look close to death. Yet I continue to keep my guard up, because appearances can be deceiving when dealing with Delanian creatures.

The arctic vampire stalks back and forth, looking at me with its red eyes like a predator. It appears to be looking for an opening in which to strike me, but I will not let it find one. Its eyes focus on the hole in my chest, but I cover that quickly.

Then the arctic vampire says, in a strange accent, "So you're one of those J bot machines I've heard so much about. You look like so much *clack* to me, hardly as impressive as the rumors made you out to be."

I run the word 'clack' through my mobile dictionary. There are no matches for that word, either in Delan or Modern Xeeonish, which means it is probably a vampiric word or possibly slang. While I do not know its exact meaning, I can derive its meaning from the context in which this arctic vampire uses it.

"I do not wish to fight you, arctic vampire," I say, my optics following its every move. "All I want to do is stay inside this cave until the blizzard passes. I won't stay here forever."

The arctic vampire shakes its head, although I am starting to think it is female based on its voice and vaguely feminine form. "No. This is *my* cave. I won it by right of conquest. Do you see those bones over there?"

The arctic vampire points at the unidentifiable pile of bones I noticed earlier. "Those belonged to the last idiot who tried to take this cave as his own. His blood tasted awful, by the way."

"I did not know this is your cave," I say. "It appeared abandoned and uninhabited to me, which is why I decided to stay here until the storm passed."

"I don't care what you did or didn't think," says the arctic vampire. She bares her long, dagger-like fangs at me. "You robots probably don't understand things like protecting territory from enemies, so you can't understand why I want to rip you to shreds right now."

I tilted my head to the side. "How do you speak Delan so

well? I thought most arctic vampires were savages incapable of speaking in anything other than hisses and growls."

"That's none of your business," the arctic vampire snaps. "The only reason I wasn't here when you got here is because I was out hunting and got caught in that terrible storm."

"So you took refuge in another cave to wait it out?" I ask.

"Of course not," says the arctic vampire. "I would have been killed by another arctic vampire. No, I just fought my way through the storm. It took me hours, but I did it."

The arctic vampire sounds proud of herself, although I find it hard to believe that any creature, even an arctic vampire born and raised in this environment, can make it through a blizzard as powerful as that one through sheer willpower. That is another hint at the strength and power of these arctic vampires, which is yet another reason to keep my guard up and not underestimate her.

"You are certainly a fearsome and brave creature if you managed to fight through that blizzard on your own," I say. "By the way, has the blizzard gone down at all since I went into sleep mode?"

"Slightly," says the arctic vampire. "But it doesn't matter because you won't live long enough to leave this place on your own two legs."

The arctic vampire lunges at me with her claws outward. I fire more finger lightning bolts at her, but then she vanishes into the shadows again.

She is gone for only a little while, however, because in the next instant she leaps out of the shadows behind me and tackles me to the floor of the cave. The impact is harder than I expected due to the arctic vampire's heavier-than-expected weight.

Still, I activate the electrical barrier in my body, which causes the arctic vampire to shriek in pain and jump off my back. I then jump to my feet and whirl around to punch her in the face, but my blow misses when she vanishes into the darkness again.

I look around again, even though I know I will not see her until it is too late. I wish I understood how her disappearance into the dark works, but even the mobile Database says that no one knows exactly how the arctic vampires do it, so I will simply have to keep my guard up as always. I cannot even sense her right now, like she has disappeared into a pocket dimension of some kind.

Then I see a flash of paleness out of the corner of my optic and I jump back just as the arctic vampire goes flying past me with her claws stretched outwards again. As she passes me, I bring both of my fists down on her body, sending her crashing into the ground.

But as soon as she hits the ground, she rolls away and jumps back to her feet. A low growl emits from her throat as she claws at the ground.

"You are stronger than you look, machine," says the arctic vampire, panting slightly. "Much stronger. When I saw the hole in your chest, I thought you were too wounded to fight. I suppose I made a mistake there."

"Yes, you did," I say. "We J bots are capable of operating even when damaged. It is nothing more than a 'flesh wound,' as I already explained to someone else today."

"Impressive," says the arctic vampire. "Most impressive indeed. I do not understand machines very well, but perhaps it would not be wise for us to keep fighting like this when it is clear neither of us will go down easily."

"You mean you do not want to fight for your territory anymore?" I ask. "Not that we actually were, of course, as I have no interest whatsoever in making your territory mine, but this does not seem like something I would expect from a vampire like you."

The arctic vampire shrugs. "While I still do not want you anywhere near my cave, I know better than to draw out a fight with someone of your strength and caliber. It would be a waste of time and energy for both of us."

The arctic vampire seems far more reasonable than she first appeared, but I do not let my guard down entirely. The mobile Database says that vampires of all stripes, including the arctic kind, are often very deceptive. She is probably saying all of this in order to get me to lower my defense, but I will, of course, not let her do that.

"If you do not want to continue the fight, then I will leave shortly," I say, glancing at the cave mouth, where I can hear the howling winds of the blizzard raging. "I do not have time to waste here in this wasteland. It is of utmost urgency that I return to Xeeo and reconnect with the Database."

"Let me guess," says the arctic vampire, scratching her chin. "You don't know how to leave these mountains, do you?"

I look at the arctic vampire. "How did you know that?"

"Because why else would you be in my cave like this if you did not already know your way around here?" says the arctic vampire. "I don't know how you got here in the first place, but I can tell you have no idea how to find the nearest Portal back to your home; otherwise, you would be long gone by now, I'm sure. Correct?"

I nod. "That is correct. Are you implying that *you* do?"

"Of course," says the arctic vampire. She pats her chest. "I was born and raised in the Winterlands. I know every inch of this place like the back of my hand. From the tip of the Frozen Peninsula to the edge of the Warmer Regions, I know it all."

My scanners indicate that she is telling the truth, although it is hard to tell for sure because my scanners are not designed to detect lies from vampires. Still, I cannot assume she is lying, because if she is telling the truth, then she seems to be my best bet for finding a way out of here and back to Xeeo. On the other hand, I cannot safely assume she is telling the truth, either, so I will have to speak carefully and make sure not to let my guard down around her.

So I say, "Are you going to tell me where the nearest Portal is, then? If so, I would greatly appreciate that."

"I will," says the arctic vampire. "But for a price."

"A price?" I repeat. "What price? I lack any digits to pay you with, as we J bots are not allowed to have money. Even if I did have some digits on hand, I know you Delanians prefer physical money over digital money, so I still wouldn't be able to pay you."

"I don't want or need *money*," the arctic vampire snorts. "Paper and metal is as useless to me as water is to you. By 'price,' I mean we will exchange services, which I can tell you robots do not have a very good understanding of."

"What services could I render to you?" I ask. "After all, as a J bot, I serve the Xeeonite public by catching criminals. I am not some profit-minded bounty hunter who hires out his services to anyone who offers him a lot of money."

"I don't need you to hunt anyone's bounty," says the arctic

vampire. "Instead, I need you to solve a problem for me and the rest of my fellow arctic vampires here, one we have not been able to solve ourselves."

"And what problem is that?" I say.

The arctic vampire points at the cave entrance. "Not far from here is a group of beings who have taken over a portion of our land and made it theirs. When they first arrived some years ago, they slaughtered dozens of arctic vampires with little difficulty, and as a result we've left them alone, even though we still do not want them here at all."

The arctic vampire sounds bitter and angry, likely due to her memories of the event. She must have been there to see it herself, which explains why she seems so strongly affected by her memories of it.

"What do these beings call themselves?" I ask. "Do you know?"

"I don't," says the arctic vampire, shaking her head. "They never introduced themselves to us. They came, staked out part of these mountains as their own, and killed any of us arctic vampires who tried to stop them. They wield magic and technology unlike anything I have ever seen and they know how to kill arctic vampires easily."

"I believe I see where you are going with this," I say. I point at myself. "You want me to go and defeat these invaders, correct? You think I can succeed where you arctic vampires failed."

"You guess correctly, machine," says the arctic vampire. "I want you to do this because you seem strong. Along with your understanding of Xeeonite technology, you might be able to put a stop to them once and for all, or at least scare them away from these mountains for a while."

"What will I receive in exchange?" I ask.

"I will show you the way to the nearest Portal," says the arctic vampire. "Then you can return to Xeeo and never have to pollute our lands with your unnatural technology again."

I consider her offer. On one hand, she might be lying in an attempt to have me lower my guard so she can kill me. On the other hand, she does not appear to be lying, although again it can be hard to tell when an arctic vampire is lying or not due to my scanners not being designed to work on them.

Her offer is good; however, I need more information on these invaders first before I agree to it. Hopefully she will be able to answer my questions about them.

"Why did these beings come and steal part of your land?" I ask. "What are they trying to accomplish?"

The arctic vampire scowls and looks away. "How should I know? They have not even tried to communicate with us. They've brought in loud, heavy machinery from your world and have dug up much of the earth and rock, but none of us vampires have ever gotten close enough to see what they are searching for. Not that I care. They stole our land and killed our brethren and that is all that matters."

Based on her description, it sounds to me like these beings might be archeologists of some sort, or maybe a mining company from Xeeo searching for mineral deposits. The Winterlands are speculated to have an immense amount of natural resources, and the only reason no one has ever succeeded in attaining these resources is because of the arctic vampires, the extreme weather, and other dangers that these mountains present to anyone who comes here. Anyone who succeeds in mining the Winterlands' natural resources will become rich; according to the mobile Database, the current value of the mountains' ores is one trillion digits.

Assuming the invaders are a profit-driven company of some sort, then it is possible they have received a license from the government of Delig to dig here. Of course, there is always the possibility that they are operating without any such license, which would make their activities illegal, which is good enough motivation for me to stop their activities right away. It might even be enough to clear my name with the Delanian authorities, which would certainly make it easier for me to return to Xeeo.

"By the way," says the arctic vampire, breaking me out of my thoughts, "if you refuse the offer, then I will kick you out of my cave and force you to wander these mountains by yourself. You might be able to find your way to the nearest village with a Portal ... or you might freeze to death, if you can even die, that is. Just something to take into consideration as you think about my offer."

I have to admit, she has a point. Without her guidance, I likely will end up freezing and being buried under the snow, lost forever. These mountains are big and easy to get lost in, even with the map in the mobile Database to guide me. It makes sense to accept this vampire's offer, then, although I keep my guard up nonetheless, just in case she is planning to betray or harm me.

So I nod and say, "All right. I will go and see what I can do about these beings, whoever they are. Will you lead me to them?"

The arctic vampire smiles. "Of course. The storm is dying down, so soon it will be safe for us to travel. We can leave in about ten minutes."

Chapter 9

Ten minutes later, just as the arctic vampire says, the blizzard is gone. I find it puzzling how quickly the blizzard disappears, but the mobile Database does say that Winterlands blizzards can leave just as quickly as they come. It is part of the unpredictability of the Winterlands, I suppose.

What is even more puzzling is how the arctic vampire predicted when it would be safe enough to travel. This may be due to her growing up here, or it may be another mysterious ability of her species. I cannot tell for sure, but it is worth noting nonetheless.

Once the arctic vampire confirms that the storm is over, she leads me out of the cave. We emerge back into the valley from before, only now the ground is covered in even more snow. It is still nowhere near as deep as the snow above, but it is slightly harder for me to traverse than it was several hours ago.

As I follow the arctic vampire to the south, I glance up at the tops of the walls around us. The sky above is still gray with clouds, although the arctic vampire assures me that it will not snow again for a few more days at least.

But the current weather conditions are hardly on the top of my list of priorities to worry about. I am more interested in finding out how the battle between the Foundation and Reunification ended or if it is still ongoing. That blizzard must have affected the course of the battle. Maybe it forced Reunification's army to retreat or maybe it helped them win.

In any case, I suppose this will not matter in the long run. Once the arctic vampire shows me where the invaders are, it will hopefully not be long before I return to Xeeo, where I can finally reunite with the Database and clear my name.

As we walk, I realize that I do not know the arctic vampire's name. It may be unimportant to know, but I like to have complete information on my allies, or at least as much information as I can realistically gather, anyway.

So I say to the arctic vampire, "I do not recall you telling me your name earlier."

"Do you *need* to know it?" says the arctic vampire without looking at me. She is a little ahead of me, moving across the snow with more grace than I.

"Technically, no," I say. "But even so, I like to know the proper names of things and people. It makes it easier to sort and search for things in my memory."

"Too bad," says the arctic vampire. "Arctic vampires do not give out their names to just anybody. You must first earn our trust, and then we give it to you."

She stops and glares at me from over her shoulder. "I thought you knew that, since you machines seem to know everything already."

"Well, we do not know *everything*," I say, stopping so I do not walk into her. "We know only as much information as has been collected by the millions of individuals across both worlds who painstakingly cataloged it for us over the century since the two worlds were connected. Besides, no one knows much about you arctic vampires anyway due to your reclusive and anti-social natures."

"We prefer to keep it that way," says the arctic vampire, turning away from me and resuming her trek across the snow-laden earth. "The rest of the world could burn for all I care, although I suppose if that happened then there would be much less blood for me to drink."

I resume walking after her, but say nothing. If she is unwilling to tell me her real name—an odd aspect of arctic vampire culture that not even the Database says anything about—then she is unwilling to tell me, plain and simple. I am not interested in forcing her to tell me; besides, from a strictly practical point of view, I do not need to know her name anyway. It is not like there are any other arctic vampires to confuse her with, anyway.

The further down this canyon that we travel, the less snow there is, until soon there is only rocky, frozen earth, with patches of snow here and there. Near the tops of the walls on either side, I spot what appear to be cave mouths and occasionally see movement within, but it is impossible to tell what creatures the movements belong to.

After about an hour or so of walking, the arctic vampire stops and says, "Did you hear that?"

I stop as well and listen. My audio receptors at first pick up nothing except the howling wind above, but soon I hear it: The sound of construction equipment—a drill, most likely—tearing through the earth nearby. I increase the range of my audio receptors and soon hear the creaking of a crane, the shouts of workers, and a minor explosion going off.

I look at the arctic vampire. "What is that noise?"

She glares at me. "The invaders, you dumb machine. They have big equipment they use to make loud noise and destroy the earth. I don't know what they're digging for, but they've been at it for months and I hear this sort of thing almost every time I come near their dig site, even in the middle of the night."

"Months," I repeat. "Well, now that I can hear them, I think I should be able to find their base on my own. You do not need to lead me any further; I can handle the rest of this journey myself."

"Fine," says the arctic vampire. She shudders. "I don't like going near those beings, anyway. They would kill me if they saw me. They always kill us."

"After I deal with them, should I return to your cave?" I say. "Or will you come to me?"

"You can return to my cave," says the arctic vampire. "After you handle these invaders, come back to my cave and I will tell you the location of the nearest Portal that will take you back to Xeeo, as part of our deal."

"I expect you to uphold your end of the agreement," I say. "Because if you do not, then I doubt either of us will be very happy about it."

The arctic vampire smiles, revealing her long, sharp fangs again. "Unlike most Delanians, we arctic vampires have little use for things like 'contracts' and 'agreements,' but I do keep my word. I guarantee it."

I nod, although I still do not trust her entirely, knowing the deceptive nature of arctic vampires. "Fine. I will make this quick because I do not want to waste any more time than I have."

I turn to resume walking, but before I do, the arctic vampire says, "Machine, wait."

I look over my shoulder at her. "What?"

"I just thought you should know that one of my fellow arctic vampires, Kalcan, is working with the invaders," says the arctic vampire. She says the name *Kalcan* like it is a slur. "He is a traitor and the only vampire those killers have ever spared. But he is also even more powerful than your average arctic vampire, so watch out."

"Why are you telling me about him?" I ask. "And why did you give me his name? I thought arctic vampires are supposed to only give out their names to those that they trust."

"Because Kalcan is a traitor," says the arctic vampire. She scoops some snow off the ground and crushes it in her hand. "He's no longer one of us. I want you to kill him if you see him. Let him know what the rest of us arctic vampires think about him working with the enemy."

She speaks so viciously that I am almost taken aback. Something about her tone tells me that this Kalcan's betrayal is more personal than she is making it out to be—maybe he had been a close friend of hers—but the exact nature of his betrayal is irrelevant to my current situation, so I do not ask about it.

I simply nod and say, "If I run into Kalcan, I will be sure to let him know your feelings about him."

"Good," says the vampire. "Now go, machine, and rid our land of these invaders, just as you promised. And if you don't, then I will get to you well before the invaders do."

I nod once more and turn to leave again before remembering

something else I need to ask her.

So I turn around once more, saying, "By the way—"

But the vampire is nowhere to be seen.

Not long after we separate, I crest a hill and discover the dig site that the arctic vampire told me about. It is a massive pit in the earth—so deep and dark that I cannot see its bottom—that appears to have been dug out by heavy machinery. It is the largest and deepest pit I have ever seen, even bigger than the ore mines north of Xeeon, which makes me wonder what these people are digging for.

But I do not really have an opportunity to look as much as I like because I am not alone here. Large machinery, such as a giant crane on the other side of the pit, is operated by dwarves, although some of the equipment is clearly automated, such as a mechanical lift that allows the workers to rise up and down the pit easily.

I crouch behind a gathering of rocks and snow as low as I can, which allows me to remain hidden from the workers while still being able to see them. That drilling sound is closer than ever and appears to be coming from the massive pit. Even so, the echoing of the sound off the pit walls and the surrounding mountains makes it impossible for me to determine the pit's exact depth.

Near the crane is a box-shaped building that is clearly meant to be temporary, based on how flimsy its materials appear. Its roof is covered with snow, although one of the dwarfish workers, armed with a shovel, is shoveling the snow off as quickly as he can.

The temperature around here is much warmer than the rest of

the mountains by at least twenty degrees, although it is hardly burning hot. I suspect that the presence of so much machinery and equipment is contributing to the warmer temperatures. Still, all of the workers are wearing thick clothes, which makes sense even with the warmer temperatures.

I search for a company logo of some kind among the equipment and the workers, but I see nothing at all. It is like they are hiding their logo to prevent anyone from identifying them, which is an illegal move under the Business Logo Act, which is supposed to punish this tendency for certain businesses to hide their logos when they are performing illegal deeds.

I am not sure that this dig is even legal. My knowledge of Delanian law is not as complete as Xeeonite law, but if these invaders do not have a permit of some sort that grants them permission to dig here, then that alone will help me take them down. Perhaps I should search for whoever is in charge here and tell them that what they are doing is illegal.

But then I remember what that arctic vampire told me earlier, about these invaders slaughtering the arctic vampires who tried to stop them. If they are willing to kill so many dozens of lives in order to secure this place, then I doubt these invaders are the kind who are afraid of one robot threatening to arrest them for their illegal behavior.

I therefore must gather as much information on them as I can first. That office building, the temporary-looking one, looks like a good place to start, as that is probably where the foreman is and where they keep all of their records on this dig and every worker who is a part of it, including any permits or licenses given to them by the government of the city of Delig or some other Delanian city.

That means I will need to sneak over there carefully, however. I cannot allow anyone to see me, otherwise they will sound an alarm and I will be found and caught. Stealth has never been my strong suit, but we J bots can be stealthy when necessary, so I will simply have to do my best.

I soon spot a route that will take me to the office building without being seen by any of the workers. Keeping as low to the ground as possible, I make my way behind the line of rock and snow leading from my current position all the way to the office building. It appears this wall is made of earth and rock dumped from the dig, although I do not stay still long enough to scan it because I do not want to waste time examining things that are irrelevant to the success of my mission.

I stop when a drone—a small, flying machine that resembles a flying security camera—soars by a little too close to my path. I crouch as low as I can behind the line of rock and snow, but I still think the drone will see me, although thankfully the drone does not fly overhead and instead goes flying in the opposite direction away from me.

Looking over the low wall, I see that there are in fact many similar drones flying around the pit, although they appear to be focusing most of their attention on the pit itself rather than on its perimeters. While I find it odd that a Delanian company uses these drones, considering how most Delanians tend to be distrustful of Xeeonite technology of any sort, it does make some sense, as these drones probably take pictures and video to allow the diggers to gain a bird's eye view of their work. No doubt they also make sure that the workers are not slacking off, in addition to keeping an optic out for anyone who should not be here, like me.

I resume walking doubled over toward the office building, although I do so more cautiously now in order to avoid being spotted by the drones. It seems unlikely that any will see me, but I am not one to take unnecessary risks, especially when these risks might end with my dismantlement at the hands of company workers who might be performing illegal activity.

Soon, I reach the end of the makeshift wall of rock and snow. Still crouching as low as I can, I am just about to make a run for the office building—which is not far from my current location—when I hear the voices of two dwarves on the other side of the wall, forcing me to stay where I am so they do not see or hear me.

"And then she said, 'What, I thought *you* were on Xeeo!'" says one of the dwarves.

As soon as he says that, his partner laughs so loudly that I wonder if it will cause an avalanche. Thankfully, however, the snow on the nearby mountains does not move.

"That's hilarious," says the other dwarf. "You should tell that to everyone else. Best joke I ever heard in my life."

"I should," says the first dwarf. "But you know, Kalcan doesn't like us telling jokes, even on our break. Lousy snow-skin just wants us to work, work, work until we're dead."

"Hey, keep your voice down," says the second dwarf, who sounds worried. "Kalcan has eyes and ears everywhere, remember? Besides, I don't mind Kalcan pushing us to work. The more we work, the closer we get to completing the Mission, which I think is more important than not being able to tell jokes, even really great jokes like the one you just told me."

"Eh, I guess you're right," says the first dwarf. "I guess there will be plenty of time for joking around when the Mission is complete. Anyway, I'm done talking. Let's get lunch."

I hear the two dwarves walk away, but do not look over the wall to see where they are going. I instead take this time to think about what they were discussing, as some of what they say does not make any sense to me.

What is the 'Mission'? I suppose it might be the company's goals, whatever those are, but they spoke about it too reverently for me to assume that that is what they mean. This 'Mission' must be highly important if Kalcan is forcing them to work without much time for breaks or jokes.

Speaking of Kalcan, he is apparently the one in charge here, if those two dwarves' conversation has any truth to it. That means that not only is he a traitor to his kind, but he is also the head of this digging company.

It seems clear to me, then, that finding Kalcan should be one of my top priorities. If I can find him, then I can make him tell me about the legality of this dig, as well as what company they work for. I might even be able to convince him and his workers to leave if they are doing anything illegal, although knowing how stubborn criminals can be, that seems unlikely.

Additionally, I wonder what that dwarf's joke was. I only got the punch line, but considering how loudly his friend laughed, I can only assume that it is a great joke. Maybe it is in *Secrets of Humor*; though I will have to check at some point later, because right now I have more important things to think about.

My main challenge now is to reach and enter that office building without being seen. The rock and snow wall I have been crouching behind does not extend all the way to that building. I will have to cross the gap between this wall and the building if I am to get there, but that also means risking one of the workers or drones seeing me as well.

The best way to do that is to create a distraction that will draw all potential eyes away from the office building. Then I will be able to dash across to the building and enter before anyone notices.

All of this would be easier if I was equipped with a stealth mode. Unfortunately, that particular piece of technology is available only to members of the Midnight Patrol Squad, of which I am not. Maybe when I get back home, I will apply for a position on the Squad so I can get that stealth mode.

In any case, I need to come up with a good distraction. If only I had a blind bomb on me, then I could throw it and distract the workers that way. Unfortunately, J bots are not allowed to carry blind bombs through Portals, because the strange properties of the Portals usually cause the bombs to explode prematurely.

I peek over the short wall again in order to see if my environment will give me any ideas for a good distraction. The crane is lowering something—another large drill, by the look of it —into the pit, while a drone nearby records the crane's actions. I also notice several dwarf workers making their way down using the lift, although there are still many workers outside of the pit where they can see me if I try to sneak across to that office building.

Pulling my head back down behind the wall, I look at the office building again. I can think of no way to distract the workers and the drones, which makes this mission much more difficult than it should be.

Maybe I can hack into one of the drones and use it to cause a distraction of some sort. That might work, seeing as these drones look similar to the kind built by Annulus Robotics, Inc., which is the company that also built we J bots. It might not be difficult to do.

Then again, hacking into any of those drones will surely draw attention to myself, especially if I fail. Besides, I have no guarantee that I can establish a connection link with any of these drones; for all I know, they are custom-made for this company, which means their software may be completely incompatible with me. I still think it is worth a shot, however, because I have no other way to make a distraction. And if I am found out, I can run, even fly, away, although that will definitely make the arctic vampire angry at me when she finds out.

Hacking into one of these drones will require that I send out a signal to whichever one is nearest. Assuming these drones are built similarly to the ones created by Annulus Robotics, Inc., then I will have to make it past the password field, as well as the firewall. In my experience, drones are generally easy to hack, which is partly why they are not in widespread use in Xeeo, although the more recent models put out by Annulus Robotics, Inc., have better security against hacking than most.

Anyway, I focus on a drone that is flying several dozen feet away from my current position; not close enough to see me, but close enough that I can try to hack it without being seen.

As soon as it is within range, I send out a connection signal to it. A moment later, the words 'CONNECTION ESTABLISHED' flash across my optics, followed by, 'USER NOT AUTHORIZED TO ACCESS DRONE.'

ALLIANCE

A password screen pops up in front of the access denied screen. I expect the password to be four characters, which is the established number of characters that all drone passwords are required to have, but instead this one requires a password with five characters.

It appears my earlier theory is correct, that these are indeed custom drones built specifically for the digging company. I do not dwell on that fact, however, because I doubt it will be long before that company finds out what I am doing and tries to stop me.

As a J bot, I have a built-in password generator, which is usually used to access criminal files and computers in order to gather evidence for a trial. It is a complicated bit of software, capable of generating millions of different passwords in minutes, so I have no doubt that it will give me the password I need quickly, no matter how obscure it is.

So I run the password generator through the password screen, but the second I do so, even before the first password is generated, a large 'WARNING! UNAUTHORIZED USER ATTEMPTING TO HACK DRONE. ALL DRONES GATHER ON HACKER'S LOCATION.'

I immediately break off the connection with the drone I am attempting to hack. My vision returns to normal just in time for me to see dozens of drones flying toward me, each one sending off an extremely loud alarm, which combined with so many drones flying together makes a deafening sound.

Seeing that my cover is broken, I stand up and make a run for it in the opposite direction away from the pit. Soon, however, the drones are upon me, flying all around me and slowing my progress considerably.

The drones swarm around me so thickly that it is hard, though not impossible, to see through them. I turn every which way, but no matter which direction I look in, the drones have blocked off every escape route. Their alarms are louder than ever, so loud that I wonder if my audio receptors will be damaged by them.

Because there are so many drones no matter where I look, some of them fly into me or bounce off my head. I dodge some of them, but they keep coming at me so that I can barely avoid even that much. It doesn't seem like they are trying to capture me, however; merely stop me until someone else comes and gets me, likely the workers.

But I am not going to let them hold me back like this. I activate my electrical barrier, only this time making sure to extend its radius by a dozen feet in order to catch all of the drones at once.

It works. When the barrier strikes all of the drones in unison, they all fall to the ground around me in a clatter of metal and plastic. I quickly raise my arms to protect my head from their fall, because despite their size, these drones are quite heavy.

In seconds, I am surrounded on every side by inactive and damaged drones, which are no longer sounding their loud alarms. A few are even smoking, which means it is unlikely they will ever see action again.

But I am not free from danger just yet. Dwarfish workers are running toward me as fast as their short legs can carry them, pointing and shouting curses at me as they do so. There are at least a dozen of these workers, with more no doubt coming on the way, and they are armed with picks and shovels and other digging equipment that, while not as effective as actual weaponry, can still harm me significantly if used against me.

I turn to run into the mountains, but before I can do so, a pale claw flies toward me from the corner of my optic. I duck and roll forward over the drones, narrowly avoiding the claw, and then, when I get back to my feet, I look to see who is trying to kill me.

It is another arctic vampire, although it is clearly not the arctic vampire from before, the one who took me here. This one is bigger and more masculine, with a clearly defined jawline, and wings that are as wide as a phoenix's. He has green eyes, an unusual eye color for an arctic vampire to have, although his lips are as red as the average vampire's. He also wears clothing, some wool pants, but besides that he is shirtless, which surprises me, considering how cold it is. Then again, he is an arctic vampire, so he is probably used to the cold.

The arctic vampire advances toward me, growling as he does so, while the dwarfish workers near the pit stop when they see him. I do not know why they stop, seeing as this vampire appears to be on their side, but I am not complaining, as it will make escaping much easier.

I begin to back up, saying as I do so, "Are you Kalcan?"

The arctic vampire nods, showing no sign of surprise at the fact that I know his name. "Indeed. And you are that stupid robot, J997, that tried to stop Jornan's earlier attempts to smuggle super speed drugs into Xeeo, yes?"

"How did you know that?" I ask. "I did not see you at the crime scene."

"Jornan and I are … friends, to put it one way," says Kalcan, flashing his fangs at me. "And we tend to talk to each other. I thought for sure that you were still with the Foundation, but I guess you must have escaped the slaughter that that battle ended up being."

"Slaughter?" I repeat, still backing up as quickly as I can. "How could you know about that battle unless … are you a member of Reunification?"

"More than a member," says Kalcan, "an Elder. But yes, I was there when we slaughtered every remaining agent there. I even got to snack on a few annoying Foundation agents myself."

If what Kalcan says is true, then that means that the Foundation lost. Of course, he may be lying, seeing as he does not strike me as an honest vampire, but I cannot say for certain if that is the case or not.

But again, it does not matter. I have no loyalty to either the Foundation or Reunification. All I wish to do is go home.

So I say to Kalcan, "Let me go. I do not wish to fight you. I only came here because of a deal I made with another member of your species. Otherwise, I would not even be here at all."

Kalcan shakes his head. "Oh, machine, I am afraid it is not that simple. While you may have no interest in fighting me, you still present a clear threat to our operations, now that you've seen our pit here and destroyed almost all of our active drones. Do you really think I will let you go after that?"

"Now? I guess not," I say, "because you seem quite eager to destroy me."

"Only because you deserve it," says Kalcan. He licks his lips. "I won't get any blood from you, but tearing you apart piece by piece will make me feel better anyway."

Just as Kalcan prepares to leap at me, a familiar voice behind me shouts, "J997!"

Before I can turn to look and see who it is, a shining, blinding light explodes behind me. The blinding light causes Kalcan to put his hands over his eyes and hiss in anger, while the dwarves cover their eyes as well.

I glance up in the direction that the light is shining from and see a woman standing on a rise above us, although the light is shining so brightly that even I cannot make out who she is exactly. Her voice sounds familiar, although I do not place it immediately.

"Come here!" says the woman, whose voice I now recognize as Palos's. "Quickly, before they recover!"

I do not hesitate to listen to her calls. I activate my boosters and go flying away from Kalcan and the dwarves, heading directly toward Palos. She dims her light so I can see her, but it is still bright enough that Kalcan and his minions are incapable of following me.

I land next to her with no problem, and as soon as I do, she shuts off the light glowing from her ring. With that light gone, I can now see her much better than before.

Palos looks similar to how I remember seeing her last, although her pointed nose appears to have been broken and hastily repaired with skyras magic and her robes have been slashed and cut in several places. She looks like she has been through a fight, which makes me wonder if she fought against Reunification at the Foundation's base. Scanners indicate that her body temperature is low, no doubt due to the coldness of the mountains, although her robes appear thicker than usual, which probably help keep her warm.

"Palos?" I say. "It has been a while since I last saw you. You

167

look terrible."

She shakes her head. "It doth not matter, machine. I will explain to ye what happened later. For now, we must—"

I hear something large flying through the air toward us. Looking over my shoulder, I see Kalcan flying up at us, apparently having fully recovered from the blinding light. He is flying at us so fast that I can barely follow his movement, although I do notice his dwarves following him from a distance.

Before I can fire my finger lightning bolts at him, Palos grabs my arm and pulls. The next instant, Kalcan, his dwarves, and the pit vanish, replaced instead by an empty, small cave—not the arctic vampire's cave from before—which has barely enough room for the two of us.

As soon as we materialize in the cave, I pull my arm out of Palos's hand and step away from her. The teleportation makes my optics blink rapidly for a moment before my focus returns, which is odd because I did not suffer from any ill effects from Delanian teleportation earlier. Perhaps Palos did not do it correctly this time.

Shaking my head, I look and see Palos sit down on the cave floor, panting and sweating. She looks tired and hungry; indeed, a quick scan of her body shows me that she has not eaten in some time. Her skyras energy level appears unusually low as well, which makes me wonder how she managed not only to create that blinding light, but also to teleport us away from the pit. She must be much stronger than she appears.

"Thank you for rescuing me, Palos," I say as I dust some snow off my shoulder that I did not notice before. "You were just in time."

ALLIANCE

Palos nods, her chest heaving up and down as she wipes sweat off her brow. "Ye ... are welcome, J997. I consider ye an ally, right now the only ally destiny has chosen to bless me with. 'Tis the only good blessing I seem to have right now."

I look around the cave as she speaks. As I noted before, it is a small cave, with nowhere as much room as the arctic vampire's cave. Its temperature is low, although not freezing low, which is due to the fire burning nearby. It is not a large fire by any means, but due to the size of the cave, it does not need to be in order to heat this place well.

I see no traces or hints of vampiric occupation, which is good because the last thing I need right now is to anger another arctic vampire. Having seen the power that Kalcan and that other arctic vampire wield, I think I can live the rest of my life without getting into a fight with another.

Looking down at Palos, I say, "Palos, what happened to you? What happened to the Foundation? How did you know where to find me?"

"To answer your last question, J997, I did not know where ye might be," says Palos, shaking her head. "When the Head told me to go and get ye from the meeting room to ensure ye would survive in the event that the base fell, I discovered ye had gone missing. 'Twas a terrible thing that drained my hope from me and made me feel awful. Finding you by that pit was as much of a stroke of luck as winning a game of roll."

"It was indeed lucky for me that you chose to go there," I say. "Anyway, Kalcan told me that the Foundation lost the battle against Reunification earlier. Is that true?"

Palos sinks her face into her hands. "It is, as much as I may

169

wish it wasn't. Reunification's attack on our base was so sudden that we barely had time to rally those agents who were not wounded or dead from the previous assault. We were utterly crushed."

"I am sorry to hear that," I say. "How many agents survived?"

"I know not," says Palos, without raising her face out of her hands. "When it became clear as a summer sky that the Foundation was lost, I ran. I know not even where the Head is, though to be honest, I wish not to know that, for she will be exceedingly angry with me for my desertion if she ever finds me again."

Palos sounds completely broken, although her attitude does not extend to me, seeing as I am a robot. Still, I understand that broken attitudes like hers can affect the effectiveness of organics in stressful situations, so I should probably find a way to cheer her up soon.

First, however, I need more information, so I ask, "After Reunification's assault on the Foundation's headquarters, what did you do then?"

"I hid in this cave," says Palos, gesturing at the small cave in which we stood. "'Twas a terrible blizzard blowing, you see, and I needed some place out of the wind and snow to hide. I chose this because it is well-hidden and hard to find if ye know not where it already is."

"After that?" I say.

"After that, I slept for hours," says Palos, still not raising her face to look at me. "I was so distraught that it was the only thing I knew to do. When I awoke, I was tired and hungry, but I did not dare leave my cave, lest Reunification's agents were searching for me nearby."

"But you did leave eventually," I say. "After all, you came and helped me, did you not?"

Palos looks up at me. Tears are running down her pale face, which makes her look even more pathetic than before. "That I did, that I did. I went out because I was so overcome with guilt over my desertion that I wanted to redeem mine self. And I decided to do that by destroying Reunification's pit, the one where I saved ye."

I sit down in order to be eye level with Palos. Humans generally do not like speaking with beings above them, so I think I can make her feel more comfortable if we are on the same level.

"Did you Foundation agents know about the pit the entire time?" I ask.

"Yes," says Palos, nodding. "We have been aware of it for some time now. We set up our own Delanian base here because we suspected that Reunification would come to this place in search of what they are looking for, although they somehow managed to sneak by without us noticing until they had already dug their pit as deeply as they already have."

"I do not understand how they managed to move in all of that heavy and loud construction equipment without you Foundation agents noticing," I say. "To me, that does not speak well of your observation methods."

"The mountains are a big place and Reunification used some kind of magic to hide from us, which we only managed to notice when the Head arrived after her stay at the Xeeonite base," says Palos. She punches the floor of the cave. "But it doth not matter much anymore. They are getting closer and closer to achieving that which they have been working toward for years. And we let them do it."

"You thought you could destroy it on your own," I say. "You thought that would redeem you for your desertion."

"Yes," says Palos. She rubs the tears out of her eyes. "Indeed. Although, in truth, I do not really think I can do it by myself. Likely I would have been torn to shreds by Kalcan or killed by his dwarves if I attempted to stop them, which is the fate I deserve for my cowardly ways."

She lowers her face into her hands again and begins sobbing loudly. I do not want her to sob like this because it makes her far less effective in helping me figure out what to do next. I should figure out a way to cheer her up.

So, consulting my electronic edition of *Secrets of Humor*, I rest one of my hands on her shoulder and say, "Palos, do you know what you call a Jikorian merchant who is willing to sell his own family for profit?"

Palos stops sobbing and looks up at me with a perplexed expression. With her nose sniffling, she says, "To me, that sounds like a monster corrupted by greed itself."

"No," I say, shaking my head. "A Jikorian merchant who is willing to sell his own family for profit is called a father of profit. Get it?"

Palos stares at me with a lack of understanding in her eyes. "No, I do not. Is that supposed to be some sort of joke?"

"Yes," I say. "Do you not find it amusing?"

Palos shakes her head. "No, I do not. I see nothing amusing in that joke."

"Hmm," I say. "Maybe it is because you are a Delanian and

therefore do not understand Xeeonite humor. The original joke was in the Jikorian language, after all, so it was probably some kind of untranslatable pun that made it funny. Or maybe I just need to work on my delivery."

Palos continues to stare at me, only now, she seems more worried for my sanity than anything. It is the same look that all of the Delanians have given me every time I tell a joke. They must not be used to a robot trying to be humorous, which makes sense, seeing as there are very few robots on Dela at all.

"Anyway," I continue, in an attempt to break the ice, "let's get back to the topic of Reunification. So you say that the Foundation's Delanian branch has been overrun and destroyed by Reunification, yes?"

"Yes," says Palos. She sniffles again. "I know not how many of my fellow agents survived the slaughter, but I guess few did. However many may have perished, I must still avenge their deaths by destroying Reunification's pit and stopping them from achieving their plans."

"I see," I say. "Well, can you tell me what Reunification is attempting to accomplish? So far, you Foundation agents have kept it a secret from me by saying that I don't need to know it."

Palos looks away from me. "I still doth not wish to tell ye, but since it seems like ye and I are the only two who can stand against Reunification now, then I suppose it is safe for me to tell ye."

She looks at me again and wipes the tears from her eyes. "Reunification wishes to reunite Dela and Xeeo as one world. By any means necessary."

I tilt my head to the side. "Reunite? That does not make any sense. Dela and Xeeo have never been one world. While the two

173

worlds do share some similarities, they have always been distinct planets with their own histories and courses of evolution. They did not become connected until Simultaneous Connection happened over a century ago."

"Nay," says Palos. "That is false. A long time ago—well before you or I were even thought of—Dela and Xeeo were once one world. Then, after some traumatic cataclysm, the one world became two, and thus they have been ever since."

"Do you have any proof of that claim?" I ask. "Because I see none."

"Ye want proof?" says Palos. "Have ye never wondered why it is that someone can travel from Dela to Xeeo and survive, or vice versa? Have ye never thought it strange that skyras exists in both worlds and can be manipulated by inhabitants of both worlds? Has it not occurred to ye to consider how odd it is that humans on both worlds are able to procreate with each other, even despite the years of separation betwixt our worlds?"

I think about that for a moment. The proofs she lists off are questions that Xeeonite scientists and Delanian wizards and witches have been debating for years, among other similar questions. Yet I still do not believe that Dela and Xeeo were once one; after all, if they were at one pointed separated, how did anyone living on those worlds at the same survive what must have been an extremely cataclysmic event? It makes no sense.

"And now Reunification wishes to reunite the worlds again," says Palos. She places her hands together. "The Foundation has been fighting them for years. We have fought at a stalemate for a long time, yet it seems like all of our hard work has become for naught, now that the Foundation is but a tiny shadow of its former self."

"Assume I believe you," I say. "Assume I believe that, at some point in the past, Dela and Xeeo were one world. Why should I help you keep them separate?"

"Machine, ye are the dullest robot I have ever had the displeasure of meeting," says Palos with a sigh. "Think about it with your mechanical brain. Both Dela and Xeeo have been separated for thousands of years; they have developed into their own distinctive, incompatible geographies. By reuniting them, Reunification risks killing billions of people and utterly destroying any chance for life on the new world they wish to create, or recreate, as is the situation."

"Of course," I say. "Now I understand. But is it even possible to reunite the worlds? To my knowledge, neither Xeeonite science nor Delanian magic can even come close to doing that."

"Ye would think not, but Reunification has worked for centuries to find a way to do it," says Palos. "And I am afraid that they have finally discovered a method that may work. Yet even if they succeed in their endeavour, billions of innocent lives on both worlds will still be lost unless we stop them."

"Is Reunification searching for that method they think might work here?" I say. "What are they digging for, exactly?"

"Yes," says Palos. "Even we at the Foundation are not entirely certain what they are looking for, but we believe they are close to finding it. They likely have a similar site on Xeeo, though where it may be, I know not."

"I know what we should do," I say. "We should go to Xeeo, where I can reconnect with the Database and share all that you told me with my fellow J bots. Then we can work with the

Knights of Se-Dela to come here and put a stop to Reunification's genocidal plans."

To me, it seems like an imminently logical plan, but Palos laughs like it is the silliest thing she has ever heard.

"What?" I say. "I did not tell a joke this time. What do you find so amusing about my plan?"

"'Tis no joke I hear in your words," says Palos, a dark chuckle coming from her mouth. "I simply believe that your plan has as much chance of working as a Diamusk vehicle without wheels. Nay, it would not work and may even spell doom for both worlds if put into action."

"Explain."

"Firstly, you are a still a wanted criminal on Dela," says Palos. "Or did ye forget that? The Knights of Se-Dela would likely demand that the Xeeonites hand ye over to them to be tried for your crimes against the Order. That by itself would delay your plan considerably, even if they discover that ye did not kill those Knights ye worked with."

"Ah, yes," I say. "I almost forgot about that."

"Furthermore," says Palos, who seems to be on a roll now, "it will take us many days to find the nearest Portal to Xeeo, even with my teleportation powers, and many more days to convince the Knights of Se-Dela that Reunification even exists. By the time we do so, Reunification could be so far ahead in their plans as to make our efforts to stop them utterly meaningless."

"That is true," I say. "We do not have all of the time in the world to do all of that. What do you suggest we do, then?"

"Go back to Reunification's pit and put an end to their evil and wicked plans once and for all," says Palos. She brushes her bangs out of her eyes. "We are the only two who are in any position to save our worlds from the destruction and tragedy that Reunification wishes to bring upon them."

I stand up to my full height and consider Palos's idea. I still do not trust the Foundation or Reunification very much, but I do trust Palos more than any of the Foundation agents I've met. And if what she says is true, then I must help her stop Reunification before they succeed in their plans.

On the other hand, Palos might very well be lying. I cannot confirm or deny this, but considering how secretive the Foundation has acted ever since I have known them, it seems unlikely to me that Palos is telling the truth. Her story about Xeeo and Dela having once been one world is also hard, if not impossible, for me to believe.

Even if her story is false, however, that does not excuse all of the wrong things that Reunification has done recently. They murdered those Knights I worked with, framed me for their murders, and murdered many Foundation agents. Not to mention they are most likely operating without a permit or license from the Deligian government out here, which is another strike against them.

As a law enforcer, it is my job to capture and bring criminals to justice. Perhaps I can even clear my name by arresting someone from Reunification and making them confess to framing me. Considering I have no other real choice in this matter, I think it is worth doing.

So I nod and say, "All right, Palos. I'll work with you to end Reunification's operations here. But first, let's take a few minutes to come up with a plan of action before we do anything else."

Chapter 10

After Palos and I come up with a plan to defeat Reunification, we set out from her cave to the pit immediately. We decide to teleport, because we do not know how close Reunification is to finding what they are looking for; therefore, we have no time to waste.

We teleport on the other side of the pit, opposite the side I was on when I first sneaked into their camp. We end up behind another pile of dirt, much larger than the one I hid behind. It is slightly covered in snow, but thankfully we are not in any danger of being spotted back here.

I peer around the side of the mound and see a large metal mine cart full of the disabled drones from before. I do not see any of the workers pushing the mine cart along, which means that it is likely simply placed here until they can take the drones to wherever they dump their garbage. Or maybe they are planning to repair them later, although considering how many of them were smoking when I short-circuited them earlier, I doubt they are in any position to be repaired by even the most skilled drone repair technicians.

But I do see some of the workers. Though they do not look like workers anymore; instead, they resemble guards, as I notice they have swords and laser guns strapped to their belts now. I am certain they did not have these weapons before, when I first came here; maybe Kalcan ordered them to carry weapons in case someone else attempts to interfere with their 'Mission,' as they call it.

Not to mention that their security does indeed appear to be upped. I see far more dwarves standing along the rim of the pit than there were before, their eyes searching the whole area as keenly as hawks, while a few dwarves stand on top of buildings and construction equipment in an attempt to give them a bird's eye view of the whole area. None of them are looking in this direction, which is good, because that makes it easier for us to do what we plan to do.

Then I take note of the crane, easily the largest machine in the area. It is currently inactive, but I imagine it can still cause a lot of damage if you push it down in the right direction. There do not appear to be any dwarves in the operator's cab, which hopefully means that there will be few deaths when we put our plan into action.

I pull my head back behind the mound and turn to look at Palos. She is rubbing the rings on her fingers, looking nervous, but I can tell she is ready to do what we need to do.

Still, I ask her, "You remember what you're supposed to do?"

Palos looks at me in annoyance. "Of course I do. Do ye think me a dumb woman, incapable of remembering what we discussed not more than five minutes ago, if even that?"

"I was simply trying to make sure that we both understand what we need to do," I say. "Now that we both know what we need to do, what do you say about starting the plan right away?"

"Are we in danger of being found out before we can complete it?" asks Palos.

"I do not think so," I say. "Most of the dwarves are watching everywhere except the crane. As long as we do not draw attention to ourselves, I think we should be able to pull off the plan without issue."

"I pray that ye are correct," says Palos. "Because if ye are not, then … well, ye know what will happen to us."

I nod. "All right. Get ready to start on my signal."

Palos nods in return and begins examining her rings and adjusting them. I do not know why she does that, as her rings appear to fit well on her fingers, but maybe she is doing this as a last minute action to make sure that her rings do not fall off or move into a position that would be awkward for her hands.

As for me, I quickly review the plan in my mind. It is simple: By destroying the crane's foundation, we hope to knock it over onto the office building, which would destroy it. And by destroying Reunification's office building, we will not only take out Kalcan and any other high-ranking Reunification members in there, but also disrupt Reunification's plan to reunite Dela and Xeeo. At least it will be disrupted long enough for us to return to civilization and get both the J bots and Knights of Se-Dela out here to finish the job.

Because the truth is, the two of us by ourselves are not enough to stop this entire operation by ourselves. The best we can do for now is disrupt it long enough for us to gather the allies we need to actually end it. I wish we could end it on our own, but logic dictates that one witch and one robot are not enough to end an operation as extensive as this all by ourselves.

"J997?" says Palos, snapping me out of my thoughts. "I am ready. Are you?"

I nod. "Of course. Get into position."

Palos gives me the thumbs up to show she understood and then vanishes before my optics. I look around the mound again, toward the crane, and see her reappear in the crane's shadow without a sound. She then crouches low at the crane's base and nods in my direction.

Now it is time for me to put my part of the plan into action. I am supposed to fly into the air and create a distraction that will allow Palos to use her rings to knock over the crane. How long will it take for Palos to do that? I do not know, but she assured me earlier that she will pour every ounce of her skyras energy into this action, so I doubt it will take much longer than ten minutes at most.

The biggest problem, of course, is Kalcan. I do not see him anywhere, but he poses the largest threat to our plan. I do not think that any of the dwarves can hope to catch me while I fly, unless they happen to have abilities I am unaware of, but Kalcan can. Kalcan's exact strength is a mystery to me, but he looks like a bodybuilder, which, in addition to his natural arctic vampire strength and flight, means he can take me down easily if he wants.

I also do a quick scan of my energy level. Right now, it is at 65%. That is enough to allow me to fly around and cause a distraction, even use my finger lightning bolts if necessary, but I doubt it is enough to allow me to dodge Kalcan for very long if he decides to come after me.

Still, Palos needs a distraction in order to destroy the crane without anyone noticing and stopping her. And it is up to me to be that distraction, as per the plan.

Putting aside all of my reservations, I activate the boosters in my feet and go soaring into the sky above the pit. Just to be certain that they will see me, I fire a finger lightning bolt at one of the dwarfish workers, striking the ground near his feet but not actually hurting him, although he jumps back and falls over onto his behind in surprise anyway.

That works well. As I fly through the sky, I see the dwarfish workers everywhere looking up and pointing at me. Some of them are unlimbering their energy rifles and taking aim, but I can tell by the way they wield those guns that they are not used to shooting them. Even if they try to shoot them, they will not hit me, because I am moving too fast to be hit.

One of the dwarves does indeed shoot at me, but his aim is off and his energy bolt goes flying well to my left. I fire back at him anyway, however, because I want to keep all eyes on me. A quick glance in the direction of the crane shows me that Palos is already using her fire to weaken the metal foundation of the crane.

Dodging another laser, I look down into the pit I am flying above. It is quite deep and dark, making it impossible for me to see what is down there, aside from the lifts and walkways built along the walls. Sensors indicate that there is an immense amount of skyras energy radiating from within, although that is hardly unusual considering all of the skyras energy that can be found beneath the surface of the earth on this world.

The dwarves continue to aim and fire at me, but it seems to

me that they are even worse as a group, because not a single one of those dwarves comes close to even grazing me. They are clearly shooting to kill, but with their poor aim, I am surprised they have not shot each other accidentally.

As I soar to the side to avoid a lucky shot, I wonder where Kalcan is. I expect him to show up any minute now, but it appears to me that he either must not know I am here or he does not care enough to come and fight me himself. Maybe he is afraid of getting hit by his dwarves who are almost literally incapable of hitting me with their lasers. Or maybe he thinks they are competent enough to take me down on their own; if so, he must not understand the competence levels of his men very well.

Then my sensors indicate something large and dangerous is coming at me from above. I look up, but do not see anything, which makes me wonder if my sensors are malfunctioning or were set off by some large bird flying nearby when something large and heavy slams into my back.

The impact almost knocks me out of the air entirely, but I manage to stay afloat even with the thing holding tightly onto my back. I fly unsteadily through the air, trying to maintain my balance, although the weight of the thing that landed on my back makes that almost impossible.

The thing is trying to push me down toward the pit, so I flip around without any warning or hesitation. The abrupt flip causes the invisible thing to let go, followed by a startled shout that sounds like Kalcan.

"I hear you, Kalcan," I call out as I turn around and look in the direction I think that the arctic vampire fell in. "Your invisibility does not fool me."

ALLIANCE

There is no answer, although I hear the sound of large wings flapping around, though they sound slightly metallic for some reason. Based on the sounds of the flapping wings, I guess that Kalcan is flying away from me. He has a little skyras energy as well; barely enough to sense, but enough for me to track his movements accurately.

I aim my fingertips and fire two electric bolts. The bolts strike the invisible Kalcan in the back, causing him to let out an oddly metallic roar in pain. He still does not appear, however, which means I will have to find a way to force him to show himself.

So I fly after him, following my scanners' skyras energy sensors. While Kalcan is a fast flier, my boosters allow me to fly even faster than he, and soon I am above the invisible vampire.

I try to punch him, but Kalcan spins out of the way and then body slams me. The blow—which feels like getting slammed by a falling boulder—sends me tumbling backwards through the air, although I manage to regain my control and balance quickly.

Shaking my head, I hear Kalcan's wings swooping through the air toward me. I aim my fingertips in his direction, but he is so fast that he is upon me before I can fire. He punches me with his fist, a blow that causes me to lose my balance and send me plummeting to the pit below us.

But I recover before I fall into the pit itself and go flying again, though I fly away from the invisible Kalcan in order to give myself a moment to think and plan. Sensors indicate that Kalcan is coming at me once more, although this time I am not going to let him hit me again.

When my sensors indicate that Kalcan is only a few dozen yards from me, I fly up abruptly. Kalcan, who is going too fast to

185

stop, ends up flying underneath me, but just as he does, I cut off my boosters and land on his back, quickly grabbing his shoulders to keep from falling off.

Strangely, my sensors indicate that Kalcan's skin is metallic, not organic, although he might be wearing some kind of armor to protect himself. In any case, that does not change what I am about to do.

With my feet on Kalcan's back, I activate my boosters, but not enough to send me flying. Instead, I make them powerful enough to cause the flames shooting out to burn my enemy.

Yet rather than hear the boiling or burning of skin under my feet, I hear the scorching of metal, followed by that strange metallic scream again. Kalcan's invisibility flickers; no, not Kalcan's, but some strange robot I have never seen before.

It is visible only for a moment, but in that moment, I see that it looks like a robotic vampire, with large metal wings and metallic skin. It most definitely does not look like armor.

Then it becomes invisible again and jerks to a stop. This sends me flying over its head, but I send more power to my boosters, allowing me to boost away safely from the robotic vampire as far from its reach as possible.

As I boost away from it, I wonder where this thing comes from and where the real Kalcan is. Why did Kalcan send this machine to fight me? Why not fight me himself?

Righting in midair, I prepare to resume my fight in the sky with the robotic vampire when the answers to those two questions occur to me immediately.

I look in the direction of the crane, where Palos is. I see Palos still melting away the foundation of the massive crane with her fire ring, which she seems to be having some progress with, as I can see she has already melted a great chunk of the foundation.

But then, from out of the shadows behind her, Kalcan emerges, his teeth bared and his claws at the ready. Palos does not appear to notice or hear Kalcan approaching behind her.

"Palos!" I shout, not caring that this might attract the attention of the workers to her position. "Kalcan is behind you!"

Palos starts when she hears me shout, but at the same time Kalcan grabs her by the shoulders from behind and throws her to the ground. Palos tries to get up almost immediately—which suggests a resilience I have not noticed in her before—but Kalcan is upon her again, only this time he grabs her hands and squeezes them inside his own.

Palos screams in pain, and then Kalcan lets go. Even from my position in the sky, I can see that Palos's fingers have been broken and bent out of shape. Most of her skyras rings have been shattered, with their remaining bits cutting into her fingers, causing them to bleed.

"Palos!" I shout again. "No!"

Kalcan stands above Palos again, flexing his powerful claws, and he picks her up. Palos kicks him in the abdomen, but Kalcan barely notices. He flashes his fangs, as if he is already imagining how Palos's blood will taste in his mouth.

I turn and zoom toward them, but then my sensors pick up the robotic vampire's skyras aura to my side. It slams into me abruptly, sending me spiraling through the sky uncontrollably. I manage to regain my balance, but as soon as I do, I hear Palos scream.

Once more, I look down toward the base of the crane. Kalcan

is digging his teeth into Palos's neck, a look of pure bliss on his features, while Palos screams and kicks at him harder than ever.

I fire my eye lasers at Kalcan, despite knowing that I am nowhere near close enough to hit him. My lasers, however, are intercepted by the robotic vampire, which briefly becomes visible again when my lasers hit it.

When the robotic vampire returns to invisibility, I can see Palos and Kalcan again. Kalcan tosses Palos to the ground. She does not move. Her neck is bloody and has two holes in it. While she is too far away for my scanners to detect, I can already tell that she is dead.

My scanners pick up the robotic vampire coming at me again. It is coming at me too fast to dodge, but I do not need to. I will end this fight now.

I fire another finger lightning bolt at the invisible machine. Sensors indicate the robotic vampire ducks to avoid the lightning bolt and changes tactics in response to my assault. Rather than come at me directly, it is going under me, like a shark attacking prey on the surface of the ocean.

My next course of action is logical: I cut off my boosters and fall toward the invisible machine. I still cannot see it, but my picture perfect memory has given me an idea of where its head is, which is all I need to know.

In less than a minute, the invisible machine slams into my gut. The impact rattles my sensors for a second before they reboot. The machine is holding me with its claws and I can hear it trying to tear me apart with its teeth.

But rather than let it do that, I activate my electrical barrier, which causes the machine to make another metallic roar. For a brief instant, the machine is visible again and now I can see its head more clearly, which resembles Kalcan's head, albeit with red eyes and a much larger mouth.

That is fine by me, because I shove my arm directly into its open mouth, between its upper and lower fangs, and shoot a finger lightning bolt into its body.

The resulting explosion sends me flying away from the creature, although I activate my boosters in time to catch myself before I can fall. As for the robotic vampire, it is no longer invisible; it is now a flaming ball of smoking metal that is falling into the pit below us. It soon vanishes from sight into the darkness.

Scanners indicate that my body suffers little negative effects from the explosion, although my right arm is inoperable thanks to taking the brunt of the blast and my armor is blackened in many areas. Nonetheless, all systems appear operational, including my boosters.

"Machine!" a familiar voice roars behind me.

I turn in time to see Kalcan flying up to me. He stops three dozen and a half feet from me, his wings beating against the air rapidly as he glares at me. His lips are even redder than before, so fresh that they glisten even without the light of the sun shining.

He wipes some of the blood off his lips and licks it off his finger before saying, "Looks like you destroyed my one and only Replica. Not that I am terribly surprised, seeing as it is experimental Xeeonite tech, but I admit to being impressed by the way you did it. Our technicians assured me that my Replica was completely invulnerable to most weapons, although I see they did not put much effort into making its interior as strong as its

189

exterior."

"How did you know Palos and I were going to come back here?" I ask.

Kalcan chuckles. "Easy. Palos is a Foundation agent, which means she is supposed to fight us and try to stop the Mission at every opportunity. As for you, I know how duty-bound you J bots are, so I surmised that you would return to arrest me as well. Having said that, however, I did not expect you to try to destroy the crane, although good try nonetheless."

"You murdered Palos," I say. "That is a crime punishable by up to a century in prison for vampires and a death sentence for any other species, according to both Xeeonite and Delanian laws on this matter."

"Laws," Kalcan sneers. "You think Reunification cares about the law? We are above the law. Our Mission is holy and must be achieved no matter how many foolish witches—or robots—we must kill to do it."

"No one is above the law," I say. "Not even we J bots are exempt from its binding."

"I don't care," says Kalcan. He bares his fangs. "You may not have any blood for me to suck, but that does not mean I cannot still turn you into scrap metal, especially when you are damaged from my Replica's explosion."

Kalcan vanishes before I can even react. In fact, when he vanishes, I cannot even sense him with my sensors. This does not make any sense, as it implies that Kalcan has no skyras energy. But if that is the case, then how is he able to accomplish so many of his magical feats?

All I know is that I must finish what Palos started. I have no time to waste fighting Kalcan. The base of the crane appears to have been melted enough that I can topple it myself, if I put enough effort into it.

So I divert all of my extra energy to my boosters and immediately go flying toward the crane. I go so fast that, even though the workers are shooting at me again, none of them even come close to hitting me. I hear Kalcan screaming at me from behind me, but I do not slow down to let him catch up.

In one minute I land on the ground. Power level is at 50% now, which is more than enough for me to do what I need to do next.

I glance at Palos's corpse briefly, which is surrounded by the broken rings, but do not dwell on it. Instead, I aim my good arm at the work she has already done, which is the melted base of the crane, and divert all energy to my left arm. Power flows through it as I charge for my most powerful finger lightning bolt yet.

I hear more screaming and look over my shoulder. The dwarfish workers are running toward me with their guns, while Kalcan is flying toward me as fast as he is able to flap his wings. I calculate that I have only three seconds before the workers get within shooting range and four before Kalcan arrives.

So I turn my attention back to the base of the crane and fire a finger lightning bolt at its base. This lightning bolt, however, is more like a lightning explosion than a bolt, because it causes an explosion that is only slightly smaller than the one caused by the Replica. The explosion throws me back onto the ground next to Palos's corpse.

Shaking my head, I look up in time to see the crane teetering back and forth, creaking loudly all the while before it finally falls to the side. It lands directly on the office building, which must have had some sort of flammable fuel in it because it causes another explosion that temporarily blocks out all other sounds in my audio receptors.

The destruction of the office building distracts the dwarves running toward me, making them go to put out the fires that have started because of it. They might also be going to look for any survivors, but that doesn't matter because I will be long gone by the time they put out the flames and rescue any survivors.

But then I realize that Kalcan is still coming at me. He does not look even slightly fazed by the explosion of the office building or the falling of the crane, although the murderous anger in his eyes is obvious even from a distance.

Rising to my feet, I check my power level again. That last blast from me took out a large chunk of my power: I am now at 35%. Enough to help me fly away, but not enough to help me fight and defeat Kalcan.

When I get to my feet, Kalcan lands opposite me and, before I can activate my boosters and escape, lashes out with a punch so fast my optics do not even pick it up. The blow crunches against my lower jaw, sending me staggering backward as Kalcan advances on me.

"You … stupid … robot," Kalcan hisses, the anger in his voice barely restrained. "You have gotten in Reunification's way one too many times now. I am done holding back. I will tear you apart into so many tiny pieces that even the best Xeeonite mechanic will be unable to put you back together."

This time, I think there may be some truth to his threat. I am too weak and damaged to fight him. I barely defeated his Replica, and that is when I was not damaged badly and had more than half energy. Any fight between him and me will inevitably end in his victory and my destruction.

Then I almost trip over something small and round. Sensors show me that it is one of Palos's rings, her gray teleportation ring by the look of it. Even though the rest of her rings are shattered, this one appears still to be in one piece.

And if it is in one piece, then it may be my only hope of survival.

I raise my left hand and fire another finger lightning bolt. Kalcan, as usual, dodges, but as he does so, I bend over and grasp Palos's gray ring in my hand. Sensors indicate it is half full of skyras energy, but that should be more than enough to help me escape.

Unfortunately, I have never used a skyras ring before, a fact which occurs to me as soon as I stand back up with the ring in my hand. Kalcan must have noticed what I grabbed, because he laughs at me.

"Did you just pick up one of Palos's rings?" says Kalcan. "What are you going to do with it, throw it at me? Robots can't use magic, you know."

Once again, Kalcan speaks the truth. The vast majority of robots on Xeeo are unable to harness the skyras energy within these rings, even though skyras energy is what fuels most of us. I do not understand why, although the dominant theory among Xeeonite scientists who study such things is that we robots lack the emotions and imagination necessary to access the energy inside the rings.

"You pathetic, walking pile of scrap," says Kalcan. "Time for you to die."

Kalcan launches himself at me. I squeeze hard on the ring, but nothing comes of it no matter how hard I try. It feels like nothing more than a useless piece of metal and stone to me, which means that my fate is indeed sealed. My only regret is that I will never be able to reconnect with the Database and share all of the new information I have learned over the past day.

But then, without warning, the ring glows in my hand. I look down at it even though Kalcan is still flying at me. It is shining just like someone is using it, which makes no sense because I do not know how to use skyras rings at all.

I have no time to dwell on it, however, because soon my whole world vanishes well before Kalcan reaches me, and I am gone.

Chapter 11

My surroundings are black nothingness for only a second. In the next, I find myself standing inside the cave that Palos and I had been in earlier, the one where we planned out our attack. Yet it now seems that I am alone in here, without Palos, the female arctic vampire from before, or anyone else.

"You are not alone, J997," says a feminine voice behind me that causes me to whirl around to see who it is.

Standing at the back of the cave is a woman in silver robes with a large swollen back that is familiar to me. Sitting beside her is another familiar man with a scarred face, as well as a female elf with a speaking snake curled around her waist. The man and the female elf are holding each other, likely to keep warm due to the coldness of the cave.

"The Head?" I say. "I did not know that you survived the attack."

The Head nods. "It was a close call, I will admit, but I did it. Reunification struck hard and fast. I only abandoned our base when it became clear that it was a totally hopeless fight."

I look down at the man and the female elf. "And Konoa and Lanresia as well? Did anyone else survive the attack?"

Konoa shakes his head. "I don't think so, although there was so much confusion that I might be wrong. As far as we know, however, we're the only three survivors of the assault, sadly enough."

I look down at Palos's ring, which is no longer glowing, and then look up at the Head again. "How did I use Palos's ring? Robots cannot use skyras rings. This makes no sense whatsoever."

The Head gestures at herself. "That would be me. I can activate skyras rings from a distance. So when I sensed that you were at the site of that Reunification pit and were in danger, I activated Palos's teleportation ring to get you out of there."

"I did not know that was possible," I say.

"For most, it is not," says the Head. "But I am a little different from most wizards, witches, and Sages."

"How did you do it?" I ask.

"I will tell you later," says the Head, although something in her tone of voice tells me that she will not. "For now, I want to thank you for disrupting Reunification's actions here. It should buy us enough time to regroup and retaliate before they can complete their Mission."

"Us?" I repeat. I point at myself. "Does that include me?"

"Of course," says the Head. "For all intents and purposes, I consider you as much a member of the Foundation as the rest of us now. You still can't go back to Xeeo, at least not right away, so you might as well stick with us."

"Especially in your current condition," says Konoa, looking at my damaged body with worry. "I'm sorry, but you look like a walking scrap heap at the moment."

"But I—" I say, before the Head interrupts me.

"You saw how cruel and vicious Reunification is," says the Head. "How they will do anything to complete their Mission, including murder innocents. Is that not enough reason for you to work with us?"

I consider the Head's reasoning. While I want to go back and report to the Database with all that I have learned, I also want to apprehend Kalcan and bring him to justice for Palos's murder. This is not simple revenge; rather, it is what I am programmed to do. And I must admit that the idea of Reunification succeeding in its Mission, with the most likely result in the deaths of billions, does bother me quite a bit.

If nothing else, I can at least stay with the Foundation's surviving members long enough for Konoa to put me back together.

So I nod and say, "All right. I will work with you three for now to defeat Reunification and arrest Kalcan for his murder of Palos. What is our first move?"

The Head smiles. That is when I notice a folded up piece of paper in the pocket of her robes, an old-looking piece of paper that seems familiar to me, but before I can look at it more closely, she stuffs it further out of sight.

"First, we need to have Konoa repair you," says the Head. "You can do that even here, right, Konoa?"

"It will be hard without all of HQ's resources," Konoa admits. "But I think I can do it if we can go to Xeeo sometime and get the spare parts and tools I need there."

"Excellent," says the Head. "And after that, we will search out the field agents; that is, those who were not at either the Delanian or Xeeonite bases during both attacks. If we are going to defeat Reunification once and for all, then we will need the help of every agent we can find."

Continues in:

Two Worlds #3:

Allegiance

Chapter One

With a hood cloaking mine face, I walked with a quickened pace through the streets of mine tiny and quaint hometown, Old Ways, located in Northern Se-Dela, far to the south of most major bustling cities and towns in this part of the country. It had been six years since I last stepped foot in this town and I had never intended to return here again, but the Mission required that I do so and I dared not go against the Mission, no matter how uncomfortable its requirements may at times be.

'Twas a quiet little town, Old Ways was. Of course, it was early morning, with the crisp cold morning air and the sun beginning to rise in the distance. Still, when I glanced up at the sky, I could see the prison of the Old Gods, also known as the moon, fading out of view. I prayed a quick prayer to the Old Gods to grant me the strength I would need for what I am about to do.

As the morning was still young, I saw no other people as I walked through the village. None of the villagers were awake;

even the animals slept. I spotted an old guard dog slumbering deeply on the front porch of a house, the creature not stirring even one inch when I passed it by. It had a bone 'tween its paws and might have been dreaming of wide open fields and playful children, though I knew not for sure, because I was not a dog.

I, too, dreamed of things. I dreamed of the day when the worlds would be one again. Dreamed of the day when the endless bickering and fighting among the peoples of Dela and Xeeo would cease. Dreamed of the day when the Mission would be complete and I and mine fellow Reunification members could rest at long last.

Most important of all, I dreamed of the day when mine siblings and me would be reunited, when we would put behind ourselves the petty arguments and silly disagreements that had ruined our relationships betwixt ourselves. As the mansion in which I grew up loomed closer and closer in mine vision, I was about to make that particular dream of mine a reality.

The mansion up ahead—tall, foreboding, and seemingly empty, although I knew that it still had within it at least one inhabitant—towered over every other hut in the village. Whereas most of the little houses here were tiny, with perhaps two or three rooms at most for a family of three or four, this mansion had three stories, with several balconies upon which I had spent many summer days as a youth sitting on, watching the prison of the Old Gods rise in the distance as day became night or playing games like flip coin with mine siblings when our parents had expressly forbid us not to.

Even so, I fingered the handle of the skyras sword sheathed at mine side. I normally was not one to use Xeeonite technology of

2

any sort, for 'twas unnatural and unwieldy in comparison to Delanian magic and equipment. Still, mine beautiful sister Kiriah had insisted I bring this blade along with me in case I should need to defend myself, although I saw no reason for it, seeing as I was not here to fight anyone.

Nonetheless, I allowed Kiriah to give me one such weapon, for after so many years apart I did not wish to ruin our brief time back together by denying her one of her requests. Besides, it reminded me of the sword I once wielded as a Knight of Se-Dela, although unlike that silver blade, this one was much lighter and allegedly superior due to its laser blade. Having not yet had a chance to test that theory, I knew not whether that was true; perhaps I would train with the sword after I completed this mission.

Soon I was climbing up the steep, narrow dirt road leading from the village up to the mansion. 'Twas not a terribly difficult climb, to be sure, as I had gone through much worse since leaving this place long ago (although due to a bout of amnesia afflicting me, I can barely remember most of it). With the sun rising in the east, I saw more and more of mine old mansion the closer I approached it.

It appeared to have been well-taken care of, for the windows reflected the rising rays of the sun as sparkling as ever, while its blue coat of paint looked as fresh as a woman's powdered nose. Most of the upper windows were shuttered, although that was clearly due to the fact that it was once night time, for even the shutters looked as beautiful as ever.

Also, the front gate—with its replica of the full moon attached on top—looked the same as it always did. A tall wrought iron fence surrounded the mansion on every side. It brought back the sweetest of childhood memories, that fence did, such as the time that mine brother and I attempted to climb over the fence when we were younglings, only for us to fall due to the sleekness of the bars. That had been the most painful day of mine young life, yet I now look upon the memory as fondly as a mother looks upon her children.

But despite how well-taken care of this place looked, I dread approaching it. For I did not only have sweet childhood memories associated with mine home; nay, I had more recent memories, the kind that I did not wish to remember, which left a sour taste on mine tongue and left my soul blacker than the heart of an arctic vampire.

Memories of fear, searching for my missing sister ... memories of anger, arguing with my brother, even punching him in the face, which 'twas a terrible memory I worked to forget, though I never truly did ... and memories of shame, memories of stomping out of that mansion and vowing never to return to this place or gaze upon the face of mine brother again.

But here I was now, striding up to the wrought iron fence, up the same path I had walked up and down on from the earliest days I could walk. The Old Gods can be humorous at times, setting aside our fates to go against our own vows. 'Twas probably the reason why mine parents always warned my siblings and I against making rash vows to the Old Gods, for they would be certain to test the truthfulness of those statements that we make in the heat of passion and anger.

I expected the gate to be locked, which would not be much of an issue as I could open it even without a key. Yet when I approached it and pressed my fingers against the cold metal, the gate swung open silently and without resistance.

This did make me hesitate. My brother, Sura, who as far as I knew still lived here, never left the gate unlocked before. This did make no sense to me. Sura was as predictable as a clock, always locking the gate when the last vestiges of the sun set and always opening it when the first rays of the sun peek over the horizon in the early morn.

Granted, the sun was indeed rising, yet this gate did not appear to have been unlocked and opened by my brother. Nay, I noticed the lock lying on the pathway, smashed off by some unknown force. This did leave me uneasy and afraid; nonetheless, I pushed the gate open entirely and stepped within the fenced area.

The front yard of the mansion looked as well-kept as the rest of mine old home. The square bushes, planted by my father even before I was born (Sura had been but a year old when they were planted), stood against the house 'neath the front windows on the first floor. The grass was trim and cut, with nary a place for any enemies or predators to hide from me.

On the right side of the yard was the full moon-shaped birdbath, which was as dry as the Dead Lands, another alarming sign to me, because brother Sura loved the tiny red wings and the sometimes large skiplegs that often came for a drink and a bath. Why would mine brother ever forget to refill the birdbath? Did make no sense to me, especially when I noticed how well-kept the rest of this place was.

The left side of the yard had the headstone of our parents, a beautifully-crafted piece of masonry again shaped like the moon when it was full in the sky. I saw nothing strange about it at first until I noticed … nay, that could not be …

I walked up to the headstone, ignoring the text written upon it, mine eyes focusing squarely on what I thought at first was an illusion, but which now I cannot deny. Just above the name of my father—FARIL, carved in large block letters—was the tiniest chipped area.

I took notice of this aberration—nay, this crime against my parents' memory—because Sura had always taken care of this headstone with great pride. Every day, after his morning duties, brother Sura would go out to this headstone and painstaking clean it, brushing out each carved letter and washing away the grime and dust which gathered upon its surface. He would even cover it with three thick woolen blankets when it hailed so as to prevent it from being damaged.

This terrible sign confirmed what I feared: Something had happened to mine brother, something that had prevented him from doing his usual duties. It had to have happened very recently, perhaps as recent as last night, for the rest of the mansion still appeared in good shape.

Hence, I drew mine skyras sword from my belt. 'Twas currently inactive, but I felt the tab I could press to make it flare to life, which I rested my thumb upon so I could use it in a pinch. I hoped to the Old Gods that I would not need to, that maybe brother Sura had been stricken with some illness that had left him bedridden, but this seemed not to me like that was the case.

Advancing toward the front door of the house, mine eyes flicker to the shuttered windows. Perhaps they were not shuttered so as to protect mine brother's privacy, but instead were shuttered to hide the evil villain who had dared to harm him. Who this was, and why they did this, I knew not; however, mine instincts told me that this must still be here, and therefore I could not let mine guard down for even a moment.

The front door of the mansion 'twas one of the few things on the house which brought me no early memories, for the old door had been replaced by a new door after it had been destroyed due to an accident I no longer recalled (although it must have been humorous, for even in this grim situation, it nearly brought a smile to mine face).

The front door looked not broken open, but I knew, from a brief alliance with a thief sometime ago, that there were ways to pick a door's lock without it appearing that it was so. When I wrapped my hand around the smooth wooden doorknob and turned it without effort, I knew someone had indeed picked it.

Yet I had no choice but to go inside if I wished to find out what happened to my brother, so I pushed the door inwards, still holding mine skyras sword at mine side. 'Twas prepared to fight to the death if necessary, for no one was allowed to harm any member of mine family, even family members I am on no good terms with.

When I opened the door, I was greeted by a familiar sickening smell: The stink of the popular drug known as super speed, which smells like smoke and mud. I recognize the stink because I was one a dealer of the super speed drug between the time I left home and the time I became a Knight of Se-Dela. 'Tis a stink ye never forget, for there is an addictive quality to it even to those such as myself, who never became addicted to the drug which we sold to the poor souls who devoured it like candy.

This alarmed me greatly, for brother Sura never used super speed drugs. As a priest of the Old Gods, Sura was forbidden to use any sort of drug that might affect his clear mind and good judgment. Did seem unlikely to me that my brother would ever even allow a user into this mansion, even if that user were a homeless and wounded traveler with no family with which to stay.

The entryway was almost pitch black, though I caught a whiff of a nearby candle that had been put out somewhat recently. Still, I did not need light to find mine way around, for I knew this mansion like the back of mine hand. I knew that to my right 'twas a wooden rack, built by our father years ago, for our shoes, under mine feet was a carpet meant to catch the mud and dirt on the soles of my shoes, and a coat rack was to my left opposite the shoe rack. I also knew that directly ahead of me was the foyer, with the stairs leading up and up to the upper floors and doors along the hall that led to other rooms.

Yet I hesitated, my hand still upon the doorknob, mine eyes scanning the shadows for even the tiniest hint of danger. The light from the sun outside illuminated the entryway enough to show me that there was no one waiting in hiding to kill me. Even so, the mansion was eerily quiet, even for Sura, who while not as boisterous as I, still made much more sound than was present in this place.

Should I leave? Or call for help? Kiriah had given me a messenger device, which currently was in my left pocket, to use to contact nearby Reunification members in case of an emergency. 'Twas a useless little thing, for I despised most Xeeonite tech, but as with mine skyras sword, I had taken it because Kiriah had insisted I take it.

On the other hand, however, I did not need think I needed aid. While Sura's disappearance was troubling, I saw no sign to suggest that many beings have invaded our home. At most, three villains may have ambushed my brother in his home, and I was more than capable of handling three villains on my own, no matter how tough they may be.

So I gently closed the door behind me, without saying a word, and then advanced slowly toward the stairs. Mine instincts suggested that Sura was likely in his room on the second floor, which was usually were he breakfasted. Besides, I did not smell the scent of cream and bread that my brother usually ate for breakfast every morning. All I smelt was the stink of super speed, which made me all the more eager to reunite with mine brother.

With every step I took, I fully expected to be attacked by whomever had came here, although nothing emerged from the darkness to injure me. It occurred to me that it was possible that whoever had assaulted mine brother was already long gone, but that did not seem likely to me. If that were so, I would have heard Sura calling for help or demanding to know who had entered his house.

Nay; whoever had assaulted mine brother was still here. Perhaps they were not on the first floor, but that did not mean I had the luxury of letting my guard down. My foes likely expected me to walk in as mindless as a toad, though they underestimated mine intelligence and tenacity for sure.

Whenever I passed a door, I would press mine ear against its surface and listen as closely as I could. Every time, I heard nothing at all on the other side of the door, which made this action of mine seem fruitless, although I continued to do it anyway just to be thorough.

Soon, however, it became abundantly clear to me that this first floor was abandoned. I was the only being down here, no doubt, which meant that I would need to climb the stairs to the upper floors in order to find my brother.

As silently as I could (though 'twas likely a fruitless gesture, seeing as my foes above probably already knew I was here), I climbed the stairs, which creaked not under my weight, for these stairs were sturdy and had withstood the pressure of three rambunctious young children for three full decades without breaking. Like with the rest of this mansion, I had fond memories of these stairs, but I could not focus on them at the moment, for I could not afford to be distracted when there was danger in this house.

After every step, I paused for a brief second to listen for the sounds of anyone above. I heard nothing, which did not reassure me much at all. Nay, it succeeded only in increasing my anxiety and tension, for I was now beginning to wonder if Sura were alive at all. I wished Kiriah were with me; as my sister, she always knew how to calm my fears, although I knew that as the Leader of Reunification, she had many important issues to deal with while I was away and therefore could not come with me even to see our older brother again.

Soon, I reached the top of the stairs, which opened out onto the second floor hall. 'Twas slightly lighter up here than it was done there; a handful of tiny candles, which smelled like blueberries, lit the area, although not enough for me to tell if any adversaries of mine lurked within the shadows.

ALLEGIANCE

Then I heard a loud *thump* and I immediately jumped. I also pressed the tab on the handle of my skyras sword, causing its blade made of skyras energy to extend into existence. I looked around hurriedly, but see nothing that could have made that sudden *thump*. Although it at least confirmed that I was not alone in this mansion, that there was someone—or, may the Old Gods forbid, some*thing*—in here with me.

The glow of my skyras sword revealed to me a little more than the candles did. Opposite me was the self-portrait of mine father, Faril, wearing his pure white priest robes of the Old Gods, while carrying the Divine Books within his arms. He looked young in this portrait, which made sense, seeing as this had been painted years ago, when I was only a small child, but even so, his gentle black eyes looked the same as when I was grew older. Mine own mother, in fact, always used to say that my father's eyes never aged, which I now understood for perhaps the first time in my life.

But again, I returned mine attention back to my surroundings. I decided to check the second floor, seeing as that *thump* I heard earlier seemed to come from somewhere around here. Where, of course, I knew not, but I was prepared to fight if the villains who hid in the shadows should dare to show their ugly faces.

Hence, I went down the hall, in the direction I heard the *thump* come from, mine skyras sword at my side and glowing, which I decided to keep active in case the villains who had broken into mine brother's house were awaiting me in ambush.

I made my way down the hall slowly but surely, listening for any sound that would tip me off to the presence of my enemies. Unfortunately, I heard not a sound aside from mine own breathing and mine heart beating away inside mine chest, sounds which sometimes seemed to fill mine ears like an exploding cannon ball.

Then I heard another sound, one that did not come from mine own body. 'Twas the sound of someone's weight shifting, as if they had been standing in place for too many hours. Did sound like it came from a door on the right side of the hall, only a few feet ahead of me. The sound ceased quickly enough, but I made my way up to the door because I knew that that was where it came from.

I placed mine hand on the handle, but did not turn it immediately. Instead, I listened closely, as closely as I could, for any other sound on the other side. I knew not, after all, who might be waiting behind this door, whether he be friend or foe, although like before, I heard nothing at all.

Still, I could not afford to turn and leave, not so soon, so I took a deep breath, made certain that I was holding mine sword as tightly as possible, and then turned the knob and entered.

This room was well-lit in comparison to the rest of the mansion. Light from several candles illuminated the room, their combined light so bright that I had to blink several times to allow my eyes to adjust to the change in brightness. When they did, mine heart nearly failed me by what I saw.

There, on the other side of the room, sat mine brother Sura, his arms and legs bound tightly to the wooden chair he sat upon. His head rested upon his chest, making it impossible for me to see his face, although his long brown hair was messy and torn in a few places, which worried me greatly.

Brother Sura was not alone, however. Standing around him were a dozen of the deadliest-looking criminals I had ever seen in mine life. They were a motley crew—some elves, some dwarves, others human—but a fearsome one nonetheless, for each member had one red skyras ring on his index finger, rings which identified them as belonging to the Red Ring Smugglers.

I raised mine skyras sword, but then someone from behind who I could not see pushed me forward. Startled, I staggered forward in an attempt to catch my balance, but as I did so, I heard the door slam shut behind me. When I regained my balance, I looked over mine shoulder and saw that the door was closed and likely locked as well. This meant I had no avenue of escape, for there was no other way out of this room save for that door.

Yet I did not allow this to panic me, even though internally I cursed these criminals to the Old Gods for their treachery. Instead, I held my skyras sword close, in the way Sir Lockfried trained me to wield mine weapon in the face of numerous enemies, as I turned to face the Smugglers again.

"Foul criminals," I said, making no effort to hide the hatred and distaste in my voice. "Unhand my brother, or be prepared to live the rest of your rotten lives without your index fingers."

One of the smugglers stepped forward. 'Twas an elfish woman, with long blonde hair done in elven braids and a short elven blade sheathed at her side, but despite her beauty, I knew her well enough to see the evil lurking within her pitiless soul.

"Apakerec," said the elvish woman, flashing a smile at me, although I knew she was not happy to see me. "Long time, no see."

I gritted my teeth, for I remembered well this wicked woman and was not fooled by her friendly tone of voice. "I wish it had been longer, Orelia."

13

She did not look much offended by my words, although when she spoke, she placed her hands over her heart and put a show of pain. "I am hurt. You and I used to be so close when you were a Smuggler. Don't you remember? I even recruited you into the organization."

"On the basis that ye could help me find my long lost sister, ye wench," I snapped. "Which, I will remind thee, ye failed to do. All ye had me do was break the law and operate under the cloak of secrecy in order to keep the Knights of Se-Dela from arresting ye, which they had every right to do."

Orelia's hands fell to her side and a sneer appeared on her face. "Right. I forgot how stupid you sound when you talk. You sound like you just walked out of an ancient storybook."

"I speak the High Tongue of mine forefathers," I replied, "which I have inherited along with mine brother and sister."

"The High Tongue." Orelia laughed. "I notice how you use 'my' sometimes instead of 'mine.' Not very consistent, are you?"

"'Tis due to the influence of outsiders like ye," I said, somewhat shamefully. "Otherwise, I would speak a more perfect version of the High Tongue."

"Sure," said Orelia with a smirk. "Anyway, I am happy to see you, Apakerec. No deception here. After all, if you hadn't come here today, all of this planning and taking your brother hostage would have been for naught."

Mine eyes flickered over to Sura, who still had not moved so much as one inch in his seat. He was so still that I almost feared that he was dead, although when I noticed his chest rising up and down slightly, I was reassured that he was in fact alive.

"Why did ye attack my brother?" I asked, returning my

14

attention to Orelia. "He has nothing to do with ye. He is a noble priest of the Old Gods. Attacking a priest of the Old Gods is a grievous offense for which swift justice must be performed in order to correct it."

Orelia smirked. "You didn't sound so defensive of your brother when you told me about him. In fact, you were quite angry about him, if I recall correctly. Angry enough to say awful things about him that you probably would not want repeated to his face."

"I was angry," I said. "I meant none of it. Even if I did, that gives ye no right to break into my brother's house and hold him hostage on his own property. 'Tis a wicked thing, but I suppose I should not be shocked, knowing how terrible ye Smugglers are."

Orelia folded her arms across her chest. "We only roughed him up a little. Want to see his face?"

Before I could respond, Orelia snaps her fingers. One of the Smugglers—likely a new member, for I did not recognize his face —grabbed Sura's hair and jerked his head up. I grimaced upon seeing his face.

Sura's face normally looked somewhat like mine, albeit with a stronger jaw and a wider forehead. Now, however, it looked like beaten meat, with dried blood covering much that was not already split open. His nose was broken and his left eye was swollen shut. A drip of some liquid that I could not identify from a distance leaked from his nose and fell onto his lap. He did not appear to be conscious, for he failed to show any signs of recognition in his eyes when his head was raised.

"Sura," I said. I glared at Orelia. "What did ye do to him?"

"Just roughed him up a bit is all," said Orelia with a smile.

"Because Noman hasn't forgotten you, Apakerec, or how you used your knowledge of us to help the Knights of Se-Dela ruin our operations in this region."

I hesitated when she mentioned Duka Noman, the leader of the Red Ring Smugglers. 'Twas a dangerous man—not as dangerous as some, but dangerous enough that it was usually unwise to anger him. I had not expected to hear from him ever again after I joined the Knights of Se-Dela, although I perhaps should have expected he would send someone after me at some point. I simply did not expect him to send someone after Sura, however, which was the most vile and wicked thing that Noman had done to me.

"And I do not regret it," I said. "Ye must have known I was never a loyal member of your petty little criminal gang. My allegiance has always been to the Old Gods, first, and to my family, second."

"Noman doesn't really care," said Orelia, shaking her head. "He told me he wants you dead. So excuse me if I don't show much interest in your principles and goals."

"But that is why I left the Smugglers and became a Knight," I said. "The Knights of Se-Dela offered me hard evidence of the location of mine sister, evidence ye Smugglers failed to give me. Though I imagine ye must know that already, as Noman is quite the well-informed man, is he not?"

"He is," said Orelia. "About the only thing he *doesn't* know is where you've been for the past two and a half weeks. Even our contacts within the Order of the Knights of Se-Dela didn't know where you were."

I bit my lower lip. Two and a half weeks ago I had gone to

Xeeo in search of my sister ... and found not only her, but a new purpose for mine life, as well. 'Twas why I had left the Order of the Knights of Se-Dela, for there was no way that the Knights would ever understand what we at Reunification were attempting to do.

"Ye need not know of the reasons for my absence," I said, putting on a brave face so that they would not sense any weakness from me. "'Twas private business."

Orelia shrugged. "Noman doesn't really care. All he cares about is the fact that you've gone a full year now without getting killed, even though that's what a dirty traitor like you deserves."

"Yes, I did indeed find it strange how ye avoided me when I was a Knight," I said. "Why was that?"

"Because the Red Ring Smugglers can't just waltz on in and kill any Knights we want to, obviously, even with our contacts in the Order," said Orelia. Then she leaned forward. "I noticed you said '*was* a Knight.' Are you not a Knight any longer? Who are you working for now?"

"'Tis none of your business, she-elf," I said. "Or Noman's, for that matter."

Rage burned in Orelia's eyes like a blazing inferno, but then she pulled back and returned standing upright. "Fine, fine. As I said, Noman doesn't care and neither do I. The point is that we have you where we want you, which is to say, alone and unable to escape from this place."

I looked around me. I had not noticed, but as we spoke, Orelia's fellow Smugglers had been surrounding me. Some stood by the sofa, others by the bookshelves, but none of then left any openings for me through which I could escape. Even the door was blocked off by a large human man, who looked like he might have been part dwarf if his bulk meant anything.

All the while, the stink of super speed filled my nostrils, though as far as I could tell, none of these Smugglers were on the drug right now. 'Twas a tragedy; not because I liked the drug, but their staying off the drug made them much harder for me to fight.

"I still do not see why ye dragged my brother into this," I said, addressing Orelia again. "He had nothing to do with my bad mistakes, which is often what I think of ye Smugglers as. 'Tis a great injustice to beat him so."

"Because we knew you would come back to see your brother sooner or later," said Orelia. She gestured at the man holding Sura's head up, who let Sura's head fall down back onto his chest. "We originally came here because we thought your brother might know where you went, but then we decided to make ourselves at home and wait here until you decided to come by and visit him."

"Ye knew of mine ... testy relationship with mine brother," I said. "How did ye know I would ever come back?"

"We didn't," Orelia admitted. "It was more of a coincidence, really. While we were interrogating your brother, our lookout came in and said he saw you coming up to the mansion. We all hurried to hide in here so we could work together to get you when you arrived."

"I see," I said. "A devious trick of yours, though I am not shocked, for I have come to expect such deception from ye."

"Good to know you still remember us," said Orelia. "For a while there, I was starting to think that you had forgotten all about us. Glad to see that my fears were misplaced."

"It matters not whether I remember ye or whether I forget ye,"

I said. I nodded at my skyras sword, the heat of its blade rolling over mine face. "I will chop down each and every one of ye and then place your heads on the fence outside as a warning to all who would dare to harm my family."

"You certainly sound serious enough to do all of that," said Orelia. "Unfortunately for you, Noman said that we're not supposed to let you have a fair fight."

She snapped her fingers again, and the man who had grabbed Sura's head now drew a long, serrated knife from his leather holster. He then placed the knife's blade under Sura's chin, close enough that he could slit mine brother's throat if he so desired.

"You have two options," said Orelia. She held up two fingers. "One, you fight us, and we kill your brother in cold blood. We don't really have anything against him, but we know how much you care about him, so holding him hostage is quite logical, wouldn't you say?"

I gritted my teeth. "What is mine other option, wench?"

"Option number two," said Orelia. A terrible smile came over her lips. "You drop that dangerous-looking skyras sword of yours and let us tear you apart piece by piece. I would have said you should also not scream, but I know I can't really expect that from you, so I'll take what I can get."

"Vile villains," I snapped. "Monsters, the whole lot of ye. Cursed from your mother's wombs, never to—"

"Does that mean you're going with option number one?" said Orelia, interrupting me as abruptly as if I had not been talking at all. "That's what it sounds like to me. I mean, it's your choice, but that really doesn't seem like a good choice to me, at least if you give a damn about your brother's life anyway."

I held my tongue, even though I had a thousand other curses I wished to hurl at these foul criminals. But I knew from experience that the Red Ring Smugglers were not the kind of monsters to make idle threats that they failed to follow up on. Nay, the Smugglers always killed who they said they would kill. 'Tis why I always worried about them coming after me when I was a Knight of Se-Dela. Now it is clear that I should have been worrying about Sura, who is infinitely less capable of defending himself than I am of defending myself.

"Nay," I said. "I will not be going with the first option. I spoke rashly earlier."

"Option number two, then?" said Orelia. "It would be a lot more sacrificial, you know, maybe even sweet in its own way, although we elves tend to think sacrificing your life for someone else is pretty silly. Still, I know how you humans think, so I was just looking at it from your point of view."

I had forgotten how much Orelia rambled. 'Twas as annoying as a pebble in the heel of my boot, but I did not allow her rambling to distract me. For Orelia was a cunning she-elf, second only to Noman in the Red Ring Smugglers, and to let mine guard down around her for even a second was to invite death upon myself.

But I could not go with either option. I did not want Sura to die, despite our estrangement, yet I did not want to die, either, for I had a grand Mission ahead of me that I could not abandon. I wished to reunite Sura with my sister and I, and I could not do that if I were dead.

Yet, as I noted earlier, I knew that I could not count on the Smugglers bluffing. If I fought back, they would kill Sura without thinking twice about it. Even if I managed to defeat them all, Sura would still be dead. 'Twould be a pyrrhic victory, if even that.

"We're waiting for your answer, Apakerec," said Orelia. She glanced at the Smuggler holding the knife to mine brother's neck. "Or would you like us to choose for you? Personally I think option number one would be the best, as that would rid us of both of you, but—"

"I am thinking," I snapped. "Please, give me a few more minutes in which to think this over. Can ye grant me that much, at least?"

"Well … fine," said Orelia. "But only three minutes. Noman doesn't want us wasting time here, not when there are a lot of super speed shipments that need to be sent out and other enemies of his that need to be killed."

Three minutes 'twas hardly enough time for me to come up with a way out of this, but it was more than I thought she would give me, so I intended to make every second of that time count.

I looked around the room in which I stood, looking for anything that could help me discover a third way out of this predicament. Sadly, all I saw was the Smugglers surrounding me on every side, looking eager to kill me, even though I knew not one of them personally. Still, the Smugglers were a rotten bunch and took any sort of betrayal as a personal slight against them, even if the traitor in question was not intending for it to be personal.

If only there was something I could do … anything … but nay. It appeared as though I was indeed caught in a tangle, unable to escape with mine life. The Founder of Reunification would be terribly angry if I were to die, but what else was I to do? Let these beasts kill mine brother? Nay, 'twas an unthinkable idea.

Seeing as I could not think of any way out of this situation alive, I pressed the tab on mine skyras sword again, making its energy blade retract into it. I placed the weapon at mine feet and kicked it toward Orelia in order to show the Smugglers that I truly had no plans to fight back.

"Very well," I said, looking at Orelia with as much hate as I could muster, for it was all I could do now. "Ye can have me. Just spare mine brother."

"The Red Ring Smugglers always keep their word, Apakerec," said Orelia as mine skyras sword stopped at her feet. She snapped her fingers again. "Men, why don't you give Apakerec a concrete display of the Smugglers' 'no quitting' policy?"

Her fellow Smugglers did not even wait for her to finish speaking before they began to advance on me. I would have picked up mine sword and fought them all off if I had had my sword, but I did not. All I could do was stand there and hope that I would die under the first blow, as I did not wish to remain aware of the sheer pain I was likely to experience when they took mine life.

The Smugglers carried chains, knives, even swords, and more than a few had brass knuckles that turned their fists into the deadliest of weapons. Though all of them were different species, 'twas obvious how each one was looking forward to giving me the beating they believed I deserved for my crimes against them.

I lowered mine head and closed mine eyes. Still I could hear them approaching, smell the stink of super speed wafting off their bodies and breath, listen as they grunted in pleasure at the thought of killing me. I prayed a quick prayer to the Old Gods to grant me protection from the Smugglers, though I knew better than to expect it.

At that moment, however, the floor shook under mine feet. 'Twas a subtle movement, one I barely felt, but there was no mistaking it. However, I continued to think that it might have simply been the combined weight and movement of the Smugglers somehow making the floor shake when I remembered that the floors of this mansion were extremely stable and could handle far more weight than this before they would so much as stir.

Then the floor shook again and I opened mine eyes and raised mine head. I was still surrounded on all sides by the Smugglers, yet they had all stopped now and were looking around the dimly lit room in confusion. Even Orelia was looked as if she was not certain what was happening, which told me that this was no trick of the Smugglers.

"What was that?" said Orelia, the tips of her ears twitching, a sign that she was losing her cool. "An earthquake?"

"Nay," I said, shaking my head. "Northern Se-Dela has not suffered an earthquake in well over three centuries. I know not what this is."

The floor shook once more, this time so violently that I was nearly thrown off my feet. Some of the Smugglers lost their footing and fell on their behinds, while Orelia staggered over to the nearest desk and leaned against it for support. Sura, meanwhile, moved not an inch in his chair, even though a shake as violent as that should most certainly have toppled his seat.

"Must be a trick," said another Smuggler, the one in front of me. He pointed at me accusingly. "He grew up here, didn't he? I bet he's doing something to make the mansion shake so he can scare us."

"Foul villain, I am just as ignorant of the true nature of this development as ye are," I said in annoyance. "Ye give me more credit than I would ever even give to mine self."

"He's lying," said the Smuggler. He raised his knife at me, an evil smile spreading across his lips. "And I know the best way to make this stop: Kill him!"

The Smuggler leaped toward me with frightening speed, his knife coming directly for mine throat. He leaped too fast for me to react, but even if I could, I would not have been able to stop his assault, for I was unarmed and helpless.

But as it turned out, I did not need to defend myself, for a large shadowy hand launched down from the ceiling and snatched the Smuggler before he could harm me. The Smuggler had only a moment to cry out in alarm before the hand pulled him back up into the ceiling, where he vanished into the shadows.

'Twas such an unexpected action that the rest of the Smugglers stood back, fear covering each of their faces. One of the Smugglers even turned and ran for the door, but another shadowy hand shot out from the threshold, grabbed him, and dragged him into the shadows kicking and screaming. His screaming was cut off the minute he vanished in the darkness and we saw no more of him.

"What the hell is this wizardry?" said Orelia. Her cool facade had dropped away completely now; her eyes were wide, her ears twitching so fast that they were almost a blur. She had drawn her own weapon now, an elven blade, but she still resembled a frightened kitten more than a fearsome criminal. "What is this? I don't—"

Another shadow hand extended from the ceiling and grabbed at her, but Orelia slashed at it with her sword. Unfortunately for her, however, her gesture was quite meaningless, for her sword cut through the hand harmlessly, allowing the shadow hand to grab her blade and yank it out of her hands. The shadow hand immediately retracted back into the ceiling, taking her shining elven sword with it.

That did seem to be the last straw for many of her fellow Smugglers, for they dropped their weapons and ran to the walls screaming in horror. They did beat their fists and feet against the walls and door, making such racket that I could barely hear myself think. One Smuggler, a dwarf, even tried to hide under the sofa, although he was too fat and succeeded only in hiding his head under it; 'twas a useless gesture, for another shadow hand shot down from the ceiling and yanked him into the darkness before he could utter even one more word.

Orelia dashed up to me and grabbed the collar of my cloak. She brought my face up to hers, allowing me to see her pale face and smell the stink of super speed on her breath. Her eyes were slightly bloodshot, a common symptom of overuse of super speed.

"What's going on here?" Orelia demanded. "Is this some kind of trick? What are you doing?"

"She-elf, in all of the days I have lived here, I have never known my mansion could do anything like this," I said.

Another shadow hand shot down from the ceiling and grabbed one of the Smugglers by the leg. The Smuggler screamed so loudly that mine ears hurt before he was dragged upwards into the ceiling, where his scream was cut off as abruptly as that of the last screaming Smuggler who had been dragged into the darkness.

Orelia let go of my collar and pushed me back. She stepped back, fear crossing her elvish features, as she said, "Your brother must know what's going on here."

She turned and dashed over to my brother before I could say another word. Sura was still unconscious and still, but now it seemed more terrifying than sad, for I did not understand how he could remain thus in the midst of all of this chaos.

Orelia stopped in front of my brother and raised his head with one hand. She then slapped him so viciously that blood shot from his face onto the floor, which made me feel quite ill indeed.

"Wake up," Orelia demanded, her tone becoming increasingly hysterical. "Wake up, you bastard. What's going on here? Tell me!"

Over Orelia's shoulder, I saw Sura's non-swollen eye flicker open. He blinked it several times, but rather than look around this place in fear and confusion, he smiled.

"Ye ask me what is going on here, heretic?" said Sura. Even I did not find his smile very calming. "The judgment of the Old Gods, of course."

"What does that even mean?" said Orelia. She raised her hand to slap him again. "I'm not even going to ask. You're clearly behind it, so I'm going to kill—"

Yet another shadow hand shot down from the ceiling and grabbed her by her raised hand. Orelia looked at it in shock, but before she could say anything, the shadow hand yanked her up toward the ceiling, where she vanished as silently as a dying wind.

She was not the only one to disappear. More and more shadow hands appeared, grabbing the remaining Smugglers and dragging them into the darkness. Most of the remaining Smugglers struggled against the shadow hands; indeed, I would have said that their struggles were almost noble or perhaps tragic if I did not utterly loathe all of them with my very being. Good riddance, I say.

Within a few minutes, all of the Smugglers were gone. The only hints that these villains had been here at all were the dropped weapons and the strong stink of super speed, although as all of the Smugglers were no longer here, even that stink was not quite as terrible as it once was.

I stood there for a full minute, expecting the hands to return and take me, even though I now knew that Sura was indeed behind them. Yet the hands did not return and the darkness appeared as normal as ever.

Lowering my hands, I dashed over to Sura, whose head had flopped onto his chest again. I stopped briefly to pick up my skyras sword, then resumed running over to him. Pressing the tab on my sword's handle to extend the energy blade, I quickly and easily cut the ropes tying him down, which stood not a chance against the heat of my blade.

Once all of the ropes were undone, they fell to the floor. Sura also leaned forward and likely would have fallen with his ropes had I not caught him in time, holding one hand on his chest. I felt his heart beating, though not as heartily as before, and felt his lungs breathing, though again, 'twas much weaker than it normally was.

I pushed Sura back up to a sitting position. Deactivating mine skyras sword, I placed the hilt back in my robe pocket and gently lifted up Sura's face. His one good eye opened again, focusing on my face with sheer incomprehension. I saw black lines retreating from his face down his neck and under his shirt, but I understood not what those meant. His skin, too, appeared pale, like he was sickly, though whether that was due to the injuries he had sustained from the Smugglers or whether it was due to those mysterious shadow hands, I knew not.

"Brother," I said. "Do ye recognize me? It is I, Rii, your younger brother."

"Rii?" said Sura, his voice weak. Another smile crossed his lips. "Oh, Rii, how long has it been since I last saw your face? Ye remind me of our father. 'Twas so long ago that he died. So long ago."

"I know," I said. "Let me help ye. I know not exactly what those monsters did to ye, but I will do what I can to heal ye. Do ye want me to call the villager healer?"

"N-Nay," said Sura, shaking his head slightly. "I … ye can heal me yourself. 'Tis a healing kit in the—"

"In the kitchen," I finished. "Yea, brother, I remember. I will go get it as soon as I get ye to your bed. Ye need rest."

"Th-Thank ye, brother," said Sura. He sounded close to fainting. "But before ye do that, I have one last thing to share with ye."

"What is that, Sura?" I asked.

Sura coughed out some blood, which alarmed me greatly, before saying, "Those Smugglers will never bother us again."

He said that like it was a great joke, for he smiled and

28

chuckled after those words left his mouth.

Then his eye closed and the last of the black lines on his neck vanished. I could tell he had lost consciousness again, which meant I would need to get him back to his bed with haste.

Picking him up in my arms, I walked toward the door as quickly as I could, trying not to think about the horrific screams of the Smugglers as they were dragged in the darkness. I also tried to ignore the lingering stink of super speed, although I did not succeed very well in that endeavor.

-

Allegiance is now available in ebook and trade paperback wherever books are sold!

Other books by Timothy L. Cerepaka

Prince Malock World:

The Mad Voyage of Prince Malock

The Return of Prince Malock

The New Era of Prince Malock

The Coronation of Prince Malock

Mages of Martir:

The Mage's Grave

The Mage's Limits

The Mage's Sea

The Mage's Ghost

Two Worlds:

Reunification

Alliance

Allegiance

Retaliation

Standalones:

The Last Legend: Glitch Apocalypse

The above books are available in ebook and trade paperback whererever books are sold!

About the Author

Timothy L. Cerepaka writes fantasy and science-fiction stories as an indie author. He is the author of the Prince Malock World fantasy novels, the Mages of Martir fantasy novels, and the science-fantasy standalone *The Last Legend: Glitch Apocalypse*. He lives in Texas.

Read about his other books at www.timothylcerepaka.com.

www.ingramcontent.com/pod-product-compliance
Lightning Source LLC
Chambersburg PA
CBHW031322170626
46807CB00002B/532